U0084397

　　本書「四技二專 1000 字」是專門
為報考升科大四技二專的同學所編輯
的。同學學習英文最常遇到的問題，便
是字彙量不足，而字彙在英文考試的各
類題型中，一直佔有最重要的地位。本
書絕對能夠幫助同學增加字彙量，並順
利締造考試佳績。

　　為了方便同學記憶，本書特別按照
單字的詞性編排，分成名詞、動詞、形
容詞、副詞等四個部分，完全符合四技
二專統一入學試題中詞彙題的測驗原
則。同時，為幫助讀者理解字義及記
憶，每個單字皆配合實用例句，所有例
句均取自歷屆全真字彙考題。

此外，書中部分單字也加注字根字首分析，使讀者不僅能提供同學自我評量之用，更能幫助同學掌握四技二專統一入學的命題趨勢，增強應考實力。

本書每隔六頁均附有一回「自我測驗」，以加深對所學單字的印象；並更附有 **Check List**，以供同學評量對所學單字的了解程度，驗收學習效果，及增進活用單字的能力。

本書之所以完成，要感謝外籍老師 Laura，謝靜芳老師及林銀姿老師的仔細校對，封面由白雪嬌小姐設計。本書雖經多次仔細編審校對，力求正確無誤，倘若仍有疏漏之處，敬請讀者不吝批評指正。

編者　謹識

怎樣背完這本單字書

1. 到劉毅家教班登記，參加英文單字
   比賽，加深背完的決心。

2. 分音節背，23813148，這個數字如
   果分爲 2-381-3148 就容易背了。背
   英文單字也是一樣，一定要唸出
   來，否則也是會忘掉。

3. **要大量地背**，一天背 5 個，一年不
   等於 5×365，因爲背了前面會忘
   記，一天如果背 60 個，即使忘一半，
   還有 30 個。

4. 將不會背的單字，做一記號，複習
   起來就快很多，不要重複複習已會
   的單字。

5. 利用已會的單字，和不會的單字加以比較，如 accomplishment 這個字，如果知道它動詞是 accomplish，只要背 accomplish 加上 ment，就容易多了。

6. 背不起來的單字，要想辦法。可以查閱學習出版公司出版的「**字根字典**」。

7. 背單字是毅力的考驗，也是記憶力的訓練，每天嘴裡不停地背，你將沒有煩惱，精神很愉快，你會變得更漂亮，更英俊，甚至眼睛發亮，因為你有了目標，未來充滿希望。

8. 背單字剛開始的時候很慢，一但抓到訣竅，就越背越快，自己給自己計算時間，看背的速度，有沒有進步。

名　詞

accident (ˈæksədənt) *n.* 意外

Carelessness often causes *accidents* and injuries. (79 保送甄試)

accomplishment (əˈkɑmplɪʃmənt) *n.* 成就

Benjamin Franklin was a man of many *accomplishments*. (80 師大工教)

account (əˈkaunt) *n.* 帳戶

He wanted to open an *account* with the Bank of Taiwan. (78 保送甄試)

accuracy (ˈækjərəsɪ) *n.* 正確性；準確性

The basketball player is able to shoot with great *accuracy*. (89 四技二專)

achievement (ə'tʃivmənt) *n.* 成就

One of the distinguished *achievements* in President Lincoln's life was freeing the slaves. (90 科大、四技二專)

acquaintance (ə'kwentəns) *n.* 認識的人

He is only an *acquaintance*, not a close friend. (78 保送甄試)

activity (æk'tɪvətɪ) *n.* 活動

Watching television is a popular *activity* in many homes, especially in large cities.

(80 台中夜二專)

addiction (ə'dɪkʃən) *n.* 上癮；沉溺

She is worried about her son's *addiction* to video games. (89 四技二專)

addition 〔 ə'dɪʃən 〕 *n.* 除～之外

In *addition* to me, there were three other visitors. (83 保送甄試)

advertisement 〔 ͵ædvə'taɪzmənt 〕 *n.* 廣告

One of the ways by which website companies make money is from the *advertisements* that flash on the screens. (90 科大、四技二專)

advertiser 〔 'ædvə͵taɪzə 〕 *n.* 廣告客戶

There are many *advertisers* who are willing to pay a lot of money to market their products. (86 中區四技夜二專)

advice 〔 əd'vaɪs 〕 *n.* 忠告

I really appreciate your *advice*. It helps me a lot. (82 四技工專、師大工教，87 南區四技夜二專)

affection 〔 əˈfɛkʃən 〕 *n.* 感情

A home is not only a house to live in but also the center of family *affection*. (82 四技商專、彰師大)

age 〔 edʒ 〕 *n.* 時代

We are living in a computer *age*.

(86 四技工專、師大工教)

agency 〔ˈedʒənsɪ 〕 *n.* 代理商

Mary works in a travel *agency*; she loves the job very much. (87 南區四技夜二專)

agreement 〔 əˈgrimənt 〕 *n.* 一致；同意

After discussing the problem for nearly two hours, they finally reached an *agreement*.

(90 科大、四技工專)

aim 〔 ɛm 〕 *n.* 目的；志向

His *aim* to be a pilot was frustrated. (81 保送甄試)

airline ('ɛr,laɪn) *n.* 航空公司

Because the flight was delayed, the *airline* offered the passengers a free meal.

（89科大、四技工專）

alarm (ə'lɑrm) *n.* 鬧鐘

My *alarm* did not go off this morning, so I was late for school. （89技優保甄）

allergy ('ælə·dʒɪ) *n.* 過敏症

If you find that some food continues to upset you, you could have an *allergy* to that food. （88保送甄試）

allowance (ə'lauəns) *n.* 零用錢

My parents give me an *allowance* for daily expenses. （89技優保甄）

alloy (ˈælɔɪ) *n.* 合金

We mixed the two metals together to form an *alloy*. (88 保送甄試)

alphabet (ˈælfəˌbɛt) *n.* 字母系統

The Phoenician *alphabet* was the most useful method of writing ever invented.

(89 中區夜四技二專)

ambulance (ˈæmbjələns) *n.* 救護車

The injured workers were taken by an *ambulance* to the nearest hospital.

(78 師大工教，83 北區夜二專)

analysis (əˈnæləsɪs) *n.* 分析

A careful *analysis* of the substance was made in the laboratory. (78 師大工教)

animal (ˈænəml̩) *n.* 動物

The earliest form of man's wealth was *animals* and tools. (80 台中夜二專)

 自我測驗

- [ ] accident   _____
- [ ] account   _____
- [ ] accuracy   _____
- [ ] acquaintance   _____
- [ ] addiction   _____

- [ ] addition   _____
- [ ] advertisement   _____
- [ ] advice   _____
- [ ] age   _____
- [ ] agency   _____

- [ ] air   _____
- [ ] alarm   _____
- [ ] allergy   _____
- [ ] alloy   _____
- [ ] animal   _____

Check List

1. 成　就　　a _accomplishment_ t
2. 帳　戶　　a _____ t
3. 正確性　　a _____ y
4. 成　就　　a _____ t
5. 活　動　　a _____ y

6. 廣　告　　a _____ t
7. 廣告客戶　a _____ r
8. 感　情　　a _____ n
9. 一　致　　a _____ t
10. 航空公司　a _____ e

11. 過敏症　　a _____ y
12. 零用錢　　a _____ e
13. 字母系統　a _____ t
14. 救護車　　a _____ e
15. 分　析　　a _____ s

antibiotic 〔͵æntɪbaɪˈɑtɪk〕 *n.* 抗生素

The doctor prescribed an *antibiotic* for my
infection. (88 保送甄試)

apology 〔əˈpɑlədʒɪ〕 *n.* 道歉

The actress demanded an *apology* from the
newspaper for an untrue report about her
personal life. (83 保送甄試)

appetizer 〔ˈæpə͵taɪzɚ〕 *n.* 開胃菜

You must have an *appetizer* before dinner.

(82 嘉南、高屏區夜二專)

appliance 〔əˈplaɪəns〕 *n.* 用具;家電用品

Refrigerators, washing machines, toasters,
and irons are household *appliances*.

(83 保送甄試)

applicant (ˈæpləkənt) *n.* 應徵者

Displaying your knowledge about the corporation may make you stand out from other *applicants*. (82 北區夜二專)

application (ˌæpləˈkeʃən) *n.* 申請；應徵

The first step in finding a job is to fill out an *application* form. (79 彰化師大, 80 四技商專)

appointment (əˈpɔɪntmənt) *n.* 約會

If you want to see a friend, you telephone first to make an *appointment*. (79 保送甄試)

```
appoint + ment
   |        |
  指定   +   n.
```

appreciation (əˌpriʃɪˈeʃən) *n.* 感激

I wish to express my *appreciation* for your help. (80 台北夜二專)

architect (ˈɑrkəˌtɛkt) *n.* 建築師

The house was built under the careful supervision of the *architect*. (82 北區夜二專)

aspirin (ˈæspərɪn) *n.* 阿斯匹靈

You can buy *aspirin* at a drugstore. (80 四技商專)

assembly (əˈsɛmblɪ) *n.* 裝配

In making automobiles, the *assembly* line technique has been carried to its extreme.

(79 彰化師大)

assistant (əˈsɪstənt) *n.* 助手

Mr. Jones is looking for an *assistant* to help him with his work. (89 四技二專)

astronaut (ˈæstrəˌnɔt) *n.* 太空人

An *astronaut* is a person who travels in a spacesi ~~~ ′ 北夜二專)

atmosphere〔'ætməs,fɪr〕n. 大氣層

A person who travels beyond the earth's *atmosphere* in a rocket-driven capsule is an astronaut.（79 四技工專）

```
atmo + sphere
  |       |
vapor +  ball（地球四周的氣體）
```

attention〔ə'tɛnʃən〕n. 注意力

Pay *attention* to what you're doing. Don't let your thoughts wander.（79 台北夜二專）

audience〔'ɔdɪəns〕n. 觀衆

The *audience* was pleased with the excellent performance.（83 四技工專、師大工教）

autobiography〔,ɔtəbaɪ'ɑgrəfɪ〕n. 自傳

We call the story of a person's life written by himself his *autobiography*.（78 師大工教）

automation 〔͵ɔtə'meʃən 〕 *n.* 自動化

As a result of *automation,* many workers became umemployed. (83 北區夜二專)

B b

bacteria 〔 bæk'tɪrɪə 〕 *n. pl.* 細菌

（單數為 bacterium）

Many diseases are spread by *bacteria.*

(87 四技工專、師大工教)

banquet 〔'bæŋkwɪt 〕 *n.* 宴會

We will have a *banquet* at this restaurant to celebrate our victory. (89 科大、四技工專)

barber's 〔'bɑrbəz 〕 *n.* 理髮店

Peter is going to the *barber's* for a haircut.

(81 四技商專)

basement 〔'besmənt 〕*n.* 地下室

The *basement* of the house was flooded during the last typhoon. (86 四技商專、彰師商教)

behavior 〔 bɪ'hevjɚ 〕*n.* 行為

Everyone was impressed by his polite *behavior*. (89 四技二專)

belongings 〔 bə'lɔŋɪŋz 〕*n. pl.* 隨身物品

When you are ready to get off an airplane, you will be told not to forget your personal *belongings*. (85 四技商專、彰化師大)

benefit 〔'bɛnəfɪt 〕*n.* 福利；津貼

A personnel manager should give information to employees about *benefits*, vacations, and other jobs in the company.

(82 四技商專、彰化師大，88 中區四技夜二專)

# 自我測驗

- [ ] antibiotic   _____
- [ ] appetizer   _____
- [ ] applicant   _____
- [ ] appreciation   _____
- [ ] architect   _____

- [ ] assembly   _____
- [ ] astronaut   _____
- [ ] atmosphere   _____
- [ ] autobiography   _____
- [ ] automation   _____

- [ ] bacteria   _____
- [ ] banquet   _____
- [ ] behavior   _____
- [ ] belongings   _____
- [ ] benefit   _____

 **Check List**

1. 道　歉　　a _____apology_____ y

2. 家電用品　a _____ e

3. 申　請　　a _____ n

4. 約　會　　a _____ t

5. 阿斯匹靈　a _____ n

6. 助　手　　a _____ t

7. 太空人　　a _____ t

8. 大氣層　　a _____ e

9. 注意力　　a _____ n

10. 觀　眾　　a _____ e

11. 自　傳　　a _____ y

12. 理髮店　　b _____ s

13. 地下室　　b _____ t

14. 行　為　　b _____ r

15. 福　利　　b _____ t

billion (ˈbɪljən) *n.* 十億

How many people are there in the world?
It has a population of more than 5.1 *billion*.

（81 保送甄試）

birth (bɝθ) *n.* 出生

December 25 is Christmas Day. It celebrates
the *birth* of Jesus almost 2000 years ago.

（88 中區四技夜二專）

block (blɑk) *n.* 街區

His home is only about two *blocks* from the
school, but hers is much farther away.

（87 中區四技夜二專）

board (bord) *n.* 董事會

He is suppose to attend the *board* meeting.

（88 四技商專）

boredom (ˈbordəm) *n.* 厭倦

Do you know how to overcome *boredom* or
frustration? （87 中區四技夜二專）

branch 〔 bræntʃ 〕 *n.* 樹枝

There is a bird sitting on the highest *branch* of the tree. (86 四技商專、彰師薦教)

breeze 〔 briz 〕 *n.* 微風

In summer, we enjoy the cool *breeze* from the sea. (79 四技工專)

Buddhism 〔ˈbʊdɪzəm 〕 *n.* 佛教

Christianity, Islam, and *Buddhism* are the three great religions of the world. (89 四技二專)

budget 〔ˈbʌdʒɪt 〕 *n.* 預算

Paul was forced to cut his *budget* after he lost his part-time job. (86 台北夜二專)

bunch 〔 bʌntʃ 〕 *n.* 串；束

The farmer cut off the *bunches* of grapes with a small pair of scissors. (87 保送甄試)

C c

calculator (ˈkælkjəˌletɚ) *n.* 計算機

May I use your *calculator* to work out this
math problem?

（86 四技商專、彰師商教）

```
calculat  +  or
    |         |
   計算   +   物
```

calendar (ˈkæləndɚ) *n.* 日曆

Holidays are often printed in red on the
calendar. （83 四技工專、師大工教）

campaign (kæmˈpen) *n.* 活動；運動

The old man was constantly making
speeches in political *campaigns* when he
was young. （89 技優保甄）

capacity (kəˈpæsətɪ) *n.* 容量

The stadium has a seating *capacity* of
10,000 people. （89 科大、四技商、農專）

career 〔kə'rɪr〕 *n.* 職業

He has decided to take teaching as his life *career*. (84 四技商專、彰師商教)

cartoon 〔kɑr'tun〕 *n.* 卡通

After school, I go straight home and watch TV. "Snoopy" is one of my favorite *cartoons*. (89 北區四技夜二專)

cash 〔kæʃ〕 *n.* 現金

I paid by check because I did not have any *cash* with me. (82 保送甄試)

caution 〔'kɔʃən〕 *n.* 謹慎

The zookeeper approached the lion with great *caution*. (91 四技二專)

celebrity ﹝ səˈlɛbrətɪ ﹞ *n.* 名人

Tom Cruise and Michael Jackson are
celebrities. (89 北區四技夜二專)

center (ˈsɛntɚ) *n.* 中心

The typhoon's *center* is a calm area, called
the eye, that measures about 20 miles
across. (88 中區四技夜二專)

centimeter (ˈsɛntəˌmitɚ) *n.* 公分

The statistics show that the average height
of students in this university is 160
centimeters. (86 保送甄試)

century (ˈsɛntʃərɪ) *n.* 世紀;一百年

There will be major changes in climate
during the next *century*. (87 四技商專、彰師商教)

chain (tʃen) *n.* 錬子

My neighbor ties up his dog with a *chain* so that it won't run away. (87 保送甄試)

change (tʃendʒ) *n.* 零錢

I need some *change* to make a phone call.

(80 彰化師大)

charity (ˈtʃærətɪ) *n.* 慈善團體

My uncle often gives money to *charities* that help the needy. (89 北區四技夜二專)

clinic (ˈklɪnɪk) *n.* 診所

He went to the dental *clinic* to have his teeth examined. (78 師大工教)

coal (kol) *n.* 煤

Coal and oil are natural products.

(81 四技工專、師大工教)

 **自我測驗**

- ☐ billion   _____
- ☐ board   _____
- ☐ breeze   _____
- ☐ Buddism   _____
- ☐ calculator   _____

- ☐ calendar   _____
- ☐ campaign   _____
- ☐ capacity   _____
- ☐ cartoon   _____
- ☐ caution   _____

- ☐ center   _____
- ☐ centimeter   _____
- ☐ chain   _____
- ☐ change   _____
- ☐ coal   _____

 **Check List**

1. 出　生　　b ___*birth*___ h
2. 街　區　　b _____ k
3. 厭　倦　　b _____ m
4. 樹　枝　　b _____ h
5. 微　風　　b _____ e

6. 預　算　　b _____ t
7. 串　　　　b _____ h
8. 活　動　　c _____ n
9. 職　業　　c _____ r
10. 現　金　　c _____ h

11. 名　人　　c _____ y
12. 世　紀　　c _____ y
13. 慈善團體　c _____ y
14. 診　所　　c _____ c
15. 預　算　　b _____ t

cockroach ('kɑkˌrotʃ) *n.* 蟑螂

It was disgusting to find a *cockroach* in the kitchen. (89 技優保甄)

code (kod) *n.* 代碼

Don't forget to write your zip *code* before you mail the letter. (87 南區四技夜二專，89 北區四技夜二專)

colony ('kɑlənɪ) *n.* 殖民地

Hong Kong was once a British *colony*.

(87 四技商專、彰師商教)

color ('kʌlɚ) *n.* 顏色

"What is your favorite *color*?" "I like white." (81 保送甄試)

combination (ˌkɑmbə'neʃən) *n.* 結合

Hope is a *combination* of desire and expectation. (80 台中夜二專)

commerce 〔ˈkɑmɝs〕 *n.* 商業

Commerce is often said to be the exchange and distribution of goods on a large scale.

（78 四技商專）

communication 〔kəˌmjunəˈkeʃən〕 *n.* 傳播

Radio and television are important means of *communication*. （79 彰化師大）

```
communica + tion
    |          |
  溝通    +   n.
```

company 〔ˈkʌmpənɪ〕 *n.* 陪伴

I hate going out alone; I take my sister along for *company*. （86 台北夜二專）

comparison 〔kəmˈpærəsn̩〕 *n.* 比較

There is no *comparison* between these two objects. （87 中區四技夜二專）

competition 〔͵kɑmpə'tɪʃən 〕 *n.* 競爭

Students have to go through very keen *competition* in the entrance examination to get into a good school. (80 四技工專)

complaint 〔 kəm'plent 〕 *n.* 抱怨

The students are full of *complaints* about the food in the cafeteria. (81 台北夜二專)

computer 〔 kəm'pjutɚ 〕 *n.* 電腦

Banking has changed a lot in recent years. *Computers* now do much of the work that the tellers used to do. (87 中區四技夜二專)

concentration 〔͵kɑnsn̩'treʃən 〕 *n.* 專心

The child with little power of *concentration* usually has difficulties in learning.

(87 中區四技夜二專)

conclusion ﹝kən'kluʒən﹞ *n.* 結論

Scientists have to observe carefully before they make *conclusions*. (89科大、四技商專、農專)

concrete ﹝kɑn'krit﹞ *n.* 混凝土

When we build modern buildings, bridges, and highways, steel and *concrete* are indispensable. (85保送甄試)

conductor ﹝kən'dʌktɚ﹞ *n.* 列車長

The *conductor* moved through the train and collected tickets. (89技優保甄)

confidence ﹝'kɑnfədəns﹞ *n.* 信心

We have *confidence* in Steve, so we are sure that he will succeed. (80台北夜二專,86中區四技夜二專)

```
con  +  fid  + ence
 |        |       |
fully +  trust  +  n.
```

consideration (kənˌsɪdəˈreʃən) *n.* 考慮

We should take several things into *consideration* before we decide something important. (87 台北夜二專)

constituent (kənˈstɪtʃʊənt) *n.* 選民

The politician asked his *constituents* to reelect him. (88 四技二專)

consumption (kənˈsʌmpʃən) *n.* 消耗

The *consumption* of electricity is higher on hot days, when most people turn on their air conditioners. (88 科大、四技工專)

contest (ˈkɑntɛst) *n.* 比賽

I am not sure if he will win in this *contest*. I have no confidence in him. (86 中區四技夜二專)

continuation〔kən͵tɪnjuˊeʃən〕 *n.* 繼續；
延續

Continuation of my work was hard after I
had been ill for a month.（78 台北夜二專）

continuity〔͵kɑntəˊnuətɪ〕 *n.* 繼續

Here lies the great danger to the *continuity*
of our national life.（82 北區夜二專）

conversation〔͵kɑnvəˊseʃən〕 *n.* 對話

I had a long *conversation* with my friends
in the tea shop.（90 科大、四技工專）

copy〔ˊkɑpɪ〕 *n.* 複製品

This is not the original; it's only a *copy*.

（86 中區四技夜二專）

corporation〔͵kɔrpəˊreʃən〕 *n.* 公司

Those young men are organizing a
corporation to sell fruit.（87 台北夜二專）

自我測驗

☐ code _____

☐ colony _____

☐ commerce _____

☐ comparison _____

☐ complaint _____

☐ computer _____

☐ concentration _____

☐ concrete _____

☐ conductor _____

☐ consist _____

☐ consumption _____

☐ contest _____

☐ continuation _____

☐ copy _____

☐ corporation _____

 **Check List**

1. 蟑　螂　　c _cockroach_ h
2. 殖民地　　c _____ y
3. 顏　色　　c _____ r
4. 傳　播　　c _____ n
5. 陪　伴　　c _____ y

6. 比　較　　c _____ n
7. 競　爭　　c _____ n
8. 結　合　　c _____ n
9. 專　心　　c _____ n
10. 結　論　　c _____ n

11. 信　心　　c _____ e
12. 選　民　　c _____ t
13. 抱　怨　　c _____ t
14. 複製品　　c _____ y
15. 對　話　　c _____ n

counter ('kaʊntɚ) *n.* 櫃檯

In a cafeteria you choose your own food from a *counter* and carry it to your table yourself. (85 四技商專、彰化師大)

country ('kʌntrɪ) *n.* 國家

After many years abroad he wanted to return home to his *country*. (77 保送甄試)

countryside ('kʌntrɪ,saɪd) *n.* 鄉下

As the *countryside* fills up, people are becoming more aware of the need for open space. (80 台中夜二專)

creation (krɪ'eʃən) *n.* 創作；作品

Isn't this painting a *creation* of art? (79 四技商專)

creature ('kritʃɚ) *n.* 生物；動物

Africa is a paradise for wild *creatures*.

(86 中區四技夜二專)

credit ('krɛdɪt) *n.* 信用

A man of good *credit* is able to purchase or receive goods without immediate payment.

（79 四技工專，87 中區四技夜二專）

critic ('krɪtɪk) *n.* 批評家

Critics say that fast food, such as hamburgers, contain too much salt and fat.

（83 保送甄試）

crowd (kraʊd) *n.* 群眾

There was a large *crowd* at the concert last night. （87 保送甄試）

cup (kʌp) *n.* 杯子

He drinks a *cup* of milk every morning.

（81 四技工專、師大工教）

cure (kjʊr) *n.* 治療

Prevention is better than *cure*.

（86 四技商專、彰師商教）

current (ˈkɝənt) *n.* 電流

A battery is used to give us an electric *current*. (82保送甄試)

D d

dairy (ˈdɛrɪ) *n.* 乳製品

In a supermarket, the *dairy* department sells milk and milk products such as butter and cheese. (85四技商專、彰化師大，86南區四技夜二專)

deadline (ˈdɛdˌlaɪn) *n.* 截止日期

Setting *deadlines* is the best way to do things efficiently. (85四技商專、彰化師大)

decision (dɪˈsɪʒən) *n.* 決定

What you study in college may be one of the most important *decisions* of your life.

(90科大、四技工專)

decoration 〔͵dɛkə'reʃən 〕 *n.* 裝飾

They spent a lot of money on the *decoration* of their new house. (78 四技商專)

```
decorat + ion
   |       |
 裝飾   +  n.
```

dependence 〔 dɪ'pɛndəns 〕 *n.* 依賴

Our *dependence* on heaters increases as the weather gets colder and colder. (89 四技二專)

desert 〔'dɛzɚt 〕 *n.* 沙漠

It is difficult for people to live in a *desert*. (89 技優保甄)

design 〔 dɪ'zaɪn 〕 *n.* 設計

This dress is a very fashionable *design*. (89 四技二專)

desire 〔 dɪ'zaɪr 〕 *n.* 慾望;願望

Paul has a *desire* to help people. (89 技優保甄)

dessert〔dɪ'zɝt〕n. 餐後甜點

"What do we have for *dessert*?" "Ice cream."

（78 保送甄試，84 保送甄試，86 南區四技夜二專，87 四技二專）

dentist〔'dɛntɪst〕n. 牙醫

Dentists take care of people's teeth and treat diseases of the mouth.（79 四技工專）

detail〔'ditel〕n. 細節

In writing an order letter, you should be careful to give every *detail* necessary for it to be filled accurately.（84 四技商專、彰師商教）

detergent〔dɪ'tɝdʒənt〕n. 清潔劑

I suggest you try this laundry *detergent*. It's expensive, but it is more friendly to the environment.（86 台北夜二專）

determination (dɪ,tɜmə'neʃən) *n.* 決心

His *determination* to succeed overcam~ aii obstacles. (78 師大工教)

device (dɪ'vaɪs) *n.* 裝置

Many stores use electronic *devices* to protect their merchandise. (89 技優保甄)

diary ('daɪərɪ) *n.* 日記

A *diary* is a book containing a daily record of the events in a person's life. (77 保送甄試)

difference ('dɪfərəns) *n.* 不同

What is the *difference* between these two sweaters? They look the same to me. (90 科大、四技工專)

differ	+	ence
不同	+	*n.*

dimensions (də'mɛnʃənz) *n. pl.* 尺寸

The carpet is too big for the *dimensions* of this room. (87 四技商專、彰師商教)

自我測驗

- ☐ counter _____
- ☐ country _____
- ☐ credit _____
- ☐ critic _____
- ☐ cup _____

- ☐ cure _____
- ☐ dairy _____
- ☐ decision _____
- ☐ dependence _____
- ☐ desert _____

- ☐ desire _____
- ☐ dentist _____
- ☐ detail _____
- ☐ detergent _____
- ☐ diary _____

Check List

1. 鄉　下　　c _countryside_ e
2. 創　作　　c _____ n
3. 生　物　　c _____ e
4. 信　用　　c _____ t
5. 群　衆　　c _____ d

6. 電　流　　c _____ t
7. 乳製品　　d _____ y
8. 截止日期　d _____ e
9. 裝　飾　　d _____ n
10. 設　計　　d _____ n

11. 餐後甜點　d _____ t
12. 決　心　　d _____ n
13. 裝　置　　d _____ e
14. 不　同　　d _____ e
15. 尺　寸　　d _____ s

dinosaur ('daɪnə,sɔr) *n.* 恐龍

The movie "Jurassic Park" is about *dinosaurs*. (86 中區四技夜二專)

directions (də'rɛkʃənz) *n. pl.* 說明

The doctor gave me *directions* for using this medicine. (77 四技商專，87 中區四技夜二專)

director (də'rɛktə) *n.* 導演；主任

The *director* asked the actors to repeat their lines. (79 北區夜二專)

directory (də'rɛktərɪ) *n.* 電話簿

You'll find his number in the telephone *directory*. (79 師大工教)

discipline ('dɪsəplɪn) *n.* 懲罰；紀律

Our teacher likes to have *discipline* in the classroom. (89 北區四技夜二專)

discount (ˈdɪskaʊnt) *n.* 折扣

To celebrate the 20th anniversary, this
department store is selling
everything at a *discount*.

dis + count
| |
not + 計算

（80 台北夜二專）

disease (dɪˈziz) *n.* 疾病

A mosquito is a common carrier of *disease*.

（77 四技工專）

dissent (dɪˈsɛnt) *n.* 不同意；異議

The chairman will not put up with any
dissent; he expects everyone to agree with
him. （87 四技商專、彰師商教）

distance (ˈdɪstəns) *n.* 距離

When you make a long-*distance* call, you
have to dial the area code first. （89 北區四技夜二專）

district 〔'dɪstrɪkt 〕 *n.* 行政區;區域

England is divided into several *districts* that are foreign to one another.（89中區夜四技二專）

diversity 〔 daɪ'vɝsətɪ 〕 *n.* 不同;多樣性

The *diversity* of opinions helps us to understand the whole picture of that case.

（84台北夜二專）

dividend 〔'dɪvə‚dɛnd 〕 *n.* 股利

The company is issuing *dividends* to its shareholders.（87四技商專、彰師商教）

document 〔'dɑkjəmənt 〕 *n.* 文件

A birth certificate is an important *document*.

（85四技商專、彰化師大）

dragon 〔'drægən 〕 *n.* 龍

You should know that a *dragon* is just an imaginary animal.（86中區四技夜二專）

drama 〔'drɑmə 〕 *n.* 戲劇

We saw a new *drama* at the theater last night.

（89 北區四技夜二專）

dressing 〔'drɛsɪŋ 〕 *n.* 調味醬

What kind of *dressing* would you like on your salad?（88 南區四技夜二專）

drugstore 〔'drʌg‚stor 〕 *n.* 藥房

In the U.S.A., *drugstores* often also sell cosmetics, candy, magazines, etc.

（80 四技商專，88 保送甄試）

dumping 〔'dʌmpɪŋ 〕 *n.* 傾銷

Some Americans are complaining about the *dumping* of Japanese goods on the American market.（87 四技商專、彰師商教）

E e

earthquake (ˈɝθˌkwek) *n.* 地震

In those island nations, *earthquakes* happen once in a while. (87南區四技夜二專)

economics (ˌikəˈnɑmɪks) *n.* 經濟學

My major is accounting but he majors in *economics*. (80四技商專)

editor (ˈɛdɪtɚ) *n.* 編輯

The *editor* made a few changes to the reporter's story. (79北區夜二專)

effect (ɪˈfɛkt) *n.* 效果

When you take some medicine, you should pay attention to its side *effects*.

(87台北夜二專)

```
ef  +  fect
 |       |
out + make, do
```

electrician (ɪˌlɛkˈtrɪʃən) *n.* 電工

We should have an *electrician* install the wiring in the basement. (79 北區夜二專)

electricity (ɪˌlɛkˈtrɪsətɪ) *n.* 電力

It'll be very dark if there is no *electricity* at night. (83 四技工專、師大工教)

electronics (ɪˌlɛkˈtrɑnɪks) *n.* 電子學

The silicon chip has revolutionized *electronics*. (82 嘉南、高屏區夜二專，82 私醫)

element (ˈɛləmənt) *n.* 因素

Constant practice is an important *element* of developing a good speaking skill.

(85 四技商專、彰化師大)

elevator (ˈɛləˌvetɚ) *n.* 電梯

We have to take the *elevator* instead of walking up the stairs to the top of the building. (80 台北夜二專，87 中區四技夜二專，89 四技二專)

 **自我測驗**

- ☐ direction _____
- ☐ director _____
- ☐ discipline _____
- ☐ disease _____
- ☐ dissent _____

- ☐ district _____
- ☐ dividend _____
- ☐ dragon _____
- ☐ drama _____
- ☐ dumping _____

- ☐ earthquake _____
- ☐ editor _____
- ☐ effect _____
- ☐ electrician _____
- ☐ electronics _____

Check List

1. 恐　龍　　d ___dinosaur___ r
2. 電話簿　　d _____ y
3. 懲　罰　　d _____ e
4. 折　扣　　d _____ t
5. 不同意　　d _____ t

6. 距　離　　d _____ e
7. 不　同　　d _____ y
8. 文　件　　d _____ t
9. 調味醬　　d _____ g
10. 藥　房　　d _____ e

11. 經濟學　　e _____ s
12. 編　輯　　e _____ r
13. 電　力　　e _____ y
14. 因　素　　e _____ t
15. 電　梯　　e _____ r

emergency 〔ɪˈmɝdʒənsɪ〕 *n.* 緊急情況

It is important to remain calm in an
emergency. (82 嘉南、高屏區夜二專，88 南區四技夜二專)

employee 〔͵ɛmplɔɪˈi〕 *n.* 員工

My friend here is an *employee* of a trading
company. (78 台北夜二專)

employer 〔ɪmˈplɔɪɚ〕 *n.* 雇主；老闆

Everyone likes to work for Mr. Johnson.
He is a respected *employer*. (81 四技商專)

encounter 〔ɪnˈkaʊntɚ〕 *n.* 遭遇；會面

I've just had a pleasant *encounter* with my
old schoolmate. (87 四技商專、彰師商教)

end 〔ɛnd〕 *n.* 末端；盡頭

I drove for almost 15 minutes before I
realized it was a dead *end*. (87 保送甄試)

energy (ˈɛnədʒɪ) *n.* 能源

Heat and light are both types of *energy*.

（82、83 保送甄試）

engineer (ˌɛndʒəˈnɪr) *n.* 工程師

My father is a mechanical *engineer* who designs machines. （87 台北夜二專）

entertainment (ˌɛntəˈtenmənt) *n.* 娛樂

Motion pictures are the most popular and widespread form of *entertainment* in the world. （80 台中夜二專）

entrance (ˈɛntrəns) *n.* 入學

If you want to pass the competitive *entrance* examination, you have to study hard.

（80 台北夜二專）

entrepreneur 〔͵antrəprə'nɝ 〕 *n.* 企業家

An *entrepreneur* is very important in getting a business going. （82 北區夜二專）

epidemic 〔͵ɛpə'dɛmɪk〕 *n.* 傳染病

The AIDS *epidemic* began in 1981, and it has caused many people to die so far.

（89 北區四技夜二專）

epi	+	dem	+	ic
among	+	*people*	+	*adj.*

equipment 〔 ɪ'kwɪpmənt 〕 *n.* 設備

The factory is in need of a lot of *equipment*.

（84 台北夜二專）

event 〔 ɪ'vɛnt 〕 *n.* 大事；事件

The school festival and the athletic meet are the two big *events* of our school year.

（89 四技二專）

evidence (ˋɛvədəns) *n.* 證據

The judge said that there was not enough
evidence to prove that the man was guilty.

（88 北區四技夜二專）

exchange (ɪksˋtʃendʒ) *n.* 匯率

The latest rate of *exchange* between the US
dollar and the New Taiwan dollar is one US
dollar for 34.7 NT dollars. （86 四技商專、彰師商教）

excitement (ɪkˋsaɪtmənt) *n.* 興奮

I lost track of the time because of the
excitement of the game. （89 北區四技夜二專）

exhaust (ɪgˋzɔst) *n.* 廢氣

The *exhaust* from various vehicles pollutes
the air. （87 四技商專、彰師商教）

expectation (ˌɛkspɛkˈteʃən) *n.* 期望

He works very hard to live up to his father's *expectations*. (77 四技商專)

expense (ɪkˈspɛns) *n.* 費用

He paid all the school *expenses* by himself.

(78 台北夜二專，88 北區四技夜二專，88 中區四技夜二專)

experiment (ɪkˈspɛrəmənt) *n.* 實驗

We usually perform chemistry *experiments* in the science lab. (89 北區四技夜二專)

expert (ˈɛkspɜt) *n.* 專家

Mechanical engineers are *experts* in machinery. (77 四技工專)

explosion (ɪkˈsploʒən) *n.* 爆炸

Some scientists say a meteorite *explosion* killed off all the dinosaurs. (88 中區四技夜二專)

expression 〔 ɪk'sprɛʃən 〕 *n.* 辭句

"Thank you" is a very important *expression*.

（78 保送甄試）

ex	+	press	+	ion
|		|		|
out	+	壓	+	*n.*

extinction 〔 ɪk'stɪŋkʃən 〕 *n.* 絕種

Rare animals facing the danger of *extinction* should be carefully protected. （86 保送甄試）

F f

facilities 〔 fə'sɪlətɪz 〕 *n. pl.* 設施

The gym is one of the *facilities* of our school.

（88 四技二專）

faculty 〔'fækḷtɪ 〕 *n.* 能力

Mental *faculties* may fail when people get old. （84 保送甄試）

自我測驗

- ☐ employee   _____
- ☐ encounter   _____
- ☐ end   _____
- ☐ engineer   _____
- ☐ entrance   _____

- ☐ entrepreneur   _____
- ☐ event   _____
- ☐ exchange   _____
- ☐ exhaust   _____
- ☐ expectation   _____

- ☐ experiment   _____
- ☐ explosion   _____
- ☐ expression   _____
- ☐ extinction   _____
- ☐ facilities   _____

Check List

1. 緊急情況　　e __emergency__ y
2. 雇　主　　　e _____ r
3. 遭　遇　　　e _____ r
4. 能　源　　　e _____ y
5. 娛　樂　　　e _____ t
6. 入　學　　　e _____ e
7. 傳染病　　　e _____ c
8. 設　備　　　e _____ t
9. 證　據　　　e _____ e
10. 興　奮　　　e _____ t
11. 期　望　　　e _____ n
12. 費　用　　　e _____ e
13. 專　家　　　e _____ t
14. 設　施　　　f _____ s
15. 能　力　　　f _____ y

February (ˈfɛbruˌɛrɪ) *n.* 二月

The second month of the year is *February*.

（77師大工教）

fee (fi) *n.* 費用

The money paid for taking care of a building is called a maintenance *fee*. （88南區四技夜二專）

film (fɪlm) *n.* 底片

You have to put some *film* in the camera before you take pictures. （87中區四技夜二專）

flame (flem) *n.* 火焰

The *flame* of the candle was our only light when the electricity was cut off. （88四技二專）

fluency (ˈfluənsɪ) *n.* 流利

To join the world market, you need *fluency* in at least one foreign language. （89四技二專）

form〔fɔrm〕 n. 形式

Among the different *forms* of transportation, the airplane is the fastest. （80 台北夜二專，82 保送甄試）

friction〔'frɪkʃən〕 n. 摩擦

Mary and Jane are both tidy, so they share the room without any *friction*. （81 台北夜二專）

friendliness〔'frɛndlɪnɪs〕 n. 友好

He shows his *friendliness* by smiling at everyone he meets. （86 四技商專、彰師商教）

friendship〔'frɛnd,ʃɪp〕 n. 友誼

At school John formed a close *friendship* with his classmates. （86 四技商專、彰師商教）

fuel〔'fjuəl〕 n. 燃料

A car usually uses gasoline as *fuel*.

（80、83 保送甄試）

function 〔'fʌŋkʃən〕 *n.* 功能

The *function* of education is to develop the mind. (79 彰化師大)

furniture 〔'fɝnɪtʃɚ〕 *n.* 家具

We gave away our sofa because we are going to buy new *furniture*. (86 四技商專、彰師商教)

G g

gambling 〔'gæmblɪŋ〕 *n.* 賭博

Gambling eats up all his savings. (78 四技商專)

garbage 〔'gɑrbɪdʒ〕 *n.* 垃圾

I am ashamed to find that the street is covered with *garbage*. (82 保送甄試)

gasoline 〔'gæsḷ͵in〕 *n.* 汽油

A car cannot move without *gasoline*.

(77 四技工專，83 保送甄試)

goods 〔 gʊdz 〕 *n. pl.* 商品；貨物

In a stationery store, one can easily find writing *goods*, such as paper, pens, pencils, ink, envelopes, etc. (79 彰化師大)

grade 〔 gred 〕 *n.* 分數；成績

I studied hard for the final exam to acquire good *grades*. (89科大、四技工專)

graduate 〔'grædʒʊɪt 〕 *n.* 畢業生

Jack just finished high school. He is a high school *graduate*. (81 四技商專)

grasp 〔 græsp 〕 *n.* 理解力

Although John is not fluent in English yet, he has quite a good *grasp* of the language.

(79 師大工教)

gratitude (ˈgrætəˌtjud) *n.* 感激

In order to express my *gratitude*, I sent her a thank-you card and a small gift.

（89 四技二專）

greenhouse (ˈgrinˌhaʊs) *n.* 溫室

If the climate becomes too hot because of the *greenhouse* effect, life on earth can not continue to exist. （82 四技商專、彰化師大）

grocery (ˈgrosəɪ) *n.* 雜貨店

You can buy some vegetables at the *grocery* store. （86 四技商專、彰師商教）

gum (gʌm) *n.* 口香糖

Do not spit out your *gum* on the floor.

（81 四技商專）

H h

harbor 〔'hɑrbɚ〕 n. 港口

Kaohsiung has a *harbor* and wide roads — so
transportation is good. (89 技優保甄)

health 〔hɛlθ〕 n. 健康

John is never sick. He is always in good
health. (77、78 師大工教)

height 〔haɪt〕 n. 高度

John is about six feet in *height*. (80 保送甄試)

helicopter 〔'hɛlɪ,kɑptɚ〕 n. 直昇機

A *helicopter* is an airplane that can go
straight up into the air. (84 四技商專、彰師商教)

holiday 〔'hɑlə,de〕 n. 假日

This Friday was a *holiday*, and I stayed at
home all day. (77 保送甄試)

 **自我測驗**

- ☐ February _____
- ☐ film _____
- ☐ fluency _____
- ☐ friction _____
- ☐ friendship _____

- ☐ fuel _____
- ☐ furniture _____
- ☐ gasoline _____
- ☐ goods _____
- ☐ grade _____

- ☐ graduate _____
- ☐ greenhouse _____
- ☐ grocery _____
- ☐ gum _____
- ☐ health _____

 **Check List**

1. 費　用　　f _____*fee*_____ e
2. 火　焰　　f _____ e
3. 流　利　　f _____ y
4. 形　式　　f _____ m
5. 友　好　　f _____ s

6. 功　能　　f _____ n
7. 家　具　　f _____ e
8. 賭　博　　g _____ g
9. 垃　圾　　g _____ e
10. 理解力　　g _____ p

11. 感　激　　g _____ e
12. 港　口　　h _____ r
13. 高　度　　h _____ t
14. 直昇機　　h _____ r
15. 假　日　　h _____ y

hospital ('hɑspɪtḷ) *n.* 醫院

Hospitals, doctors, and nurses provide medical care. (81 保送甄試，86 四技商專、彰師商教)

housework ('haʊs,wɝk) *n.* 家事

A housewife has a lot of *housework* to do every day. (80 保送甄試)

hunting ('hʌntɪŋ) *n.* 打獵

One-third of these people make their living by *hunting*. (89 中區夜四技二專)

I i

identification (aɪ,dɛntəfə'keʃən) *n.* 身分

I lost my *identification* card yesterday.

(87 南區四技夜二專)

identity 〔 aɪˈdɛntətɪ 〕 *n.* 身分

When traveling abroad, you should carry your passport to prove your *identity*.

（89 四技二專）

imitation 〔ˌɪməˈteʃən 〕 *n.* 模仿

Joe wears long hair in *imitation* of the rock singers. （89 中區夜四技二專大）

impact 〔ˈɪmpækt 〕 *n.* 影響

Computers have a great *impact* on our lives. Nowadays almost everyone is using a computer to communicate with others.

（83、85 保送甄試）

impression 〔 ɪmˈprɛʃən 〕 *n.* 印象

In order to make a good *impression* during a job interview, you need to prepare yourself for the interview. （80 彰化師大，90 科大、四技二專）

improvement 〔 ɪm'pruvmənt 〕 *n.* 改善

There is no need for *improvement* in your
typewriting now. (89 中區夜四技二專)

impurities 〔 ɪm'pjʊrətɪz 〕 *n. pl.* 雜質

Impurities in a metal may change its melting
point. (79 台北夜二專)

income 〔'ɪn͵kʌm 〕 *n.* 收入

A person's *income* is the amount of money
that he earns for his work or business.

(84 台北夜二專)

inflection 〔 ɪn'flɛkʃən 〕 *n.* 音調之高低

Native speakers can speak the language
with the right *inflection*. (79 彰化師大)

influence 〔'ɪnfluəns 〕 *n.* 影響

Television has had a great *influence* on
young people. (84、88 保送甄試)

inhabitant 〔 ɪn'hæbətənt 〕 *n.* 居民

The *inhabitants* of Taipei complained of air pollution. (78 師大工教)

initiative 〔 ɪ'nɪʃ˷ɪ͵etɪv 〕 *n.* 主動權

If you want to talk to someone, take the *initiative* and say hello. (88 四技二專)

insect 〔'ɪnsɛkt 〕 *n.* 昆蟲

A mosquito is an *insect*. (86 四技商專、彰師商教)

insistence 〔 ɪn'sɪstəns 〕 *n.* 堅持

Despite his *insistence* that he did not take the money, we still suspect him. (91 四技二專)

inspiration 〔͵ɪnspə'reʃən 〕 *n.* 激勵

His hard work has given *inspiration* to young people. (81 台北夜二專)

instructor 〔 ɪn'strʌktə 〕 *n.* 講師

The swimming *instructor* encouraged the
new students to get into the pool. (79 北區夜二專)

instrument 〔'ɪnstrəmənt 〕 *n.* 樂器；工具

Pianos and violins are musical *instruments*.

(78 師大工教)

insulator 〔'ɪnsə‚letə 〕 *n.* 絕緣體

An *insulator* prevents electricity flowing
through it. (85 保送甄試)

insurance 〔 ɪn'ʃʊrəns 〕 *n.* 保險

The most common kinds of *insurance* are
against financial loss from fire, theft, storm,
accident, death, etc. (89 中區夜四技二專)

in	+	sur	+	ance
|		|		|
into	+	*sure*	+	*n.*

intelligence 〔ɪnˈtɛlədʒəns〕 *n.* 智能；聰明

The students were given an *intelligence* test.

（81 台北夜二專，84 四技商專、彰師商教）

intel	+	lig	+ ence
apart	+	*choose*	+ *n.*

interior 〔ɪnˈtɪrɪɚ〕 *n.* 內部；室內

The house looks nice on the outside, but the *interior* looks old and rundown. （88 保送甄試）

Internet 〔ˈɪntɚˌnɛt〕 *n.* 網路

Log on to the *Internet*, and you will find the information. （88 科大、四技工專）

interview 〔ˈɪntɚˌvju〕 *n.* 面試

Jim has been looking for a job and finally he is going to ABC Company for a job *interview*. He hopes he will get the job.

（81 四技商專，84 保送甄試）

 自我測驗

- [ ] hospital _____
- [ ] housework _____
- [ ] identity _____
- [ ] impact _____
- [ ] impression _____

- [ ] impurities _____
- [ ] inflection _____
- [ ] initiative _____
- [ ] insect _____
- [ ] inspiration _____

- [ ] instructor _____
- [ ] insulator _____
- [ ] intelligence _____
- [ ] interior _____
- [ ] interview _____

Check List

1. 打　獵　　h *hunting* g
2. 身　分　　i_____ n
3. 模　仿　　i_____ n
4. 印　象　　i_____ n
5. 改　善　　i_____ t

6. 收　入　　i_____ e
7. 影　響　　i_____ e
8. 居　民　　i_____ t
9. 堅　持　　i_____ e
10. 激　勵　　i_____ n

11. 講　師　　i_____ r
12. 樂　器　　i_____ t
13. 保　險　　i_____ e
14. 網　路　　I_____ t
15. 面　試　　i_____ w

interviewer (ˈɪntɚˌvjuɚ) *n.* 主持面試者；
接見者

At the interview, she made a great impression
upon the *interviewers* with her clear speech
and good manners. (90科大、四技二專)

intruder (ɪnˈtrudɚ) *n.* 入侵者

An *intruder* broke into their house last night.

(78保送甄試)

investigation (ɪnˌvɛstəˈgeʃən) *n.* 調查

You should conduct an *investigation* in the
true scientific spirit. (79彰化師大，88保送甄試)

investment (ɪnˈvɛstmənt) *n.* 投資

He made an *investment* of $300,000 in
iron shares. (84台北夜二專)

invitation 〔͵ɪnvəˈteʃən 〕 *n.* 邀請

I am very happy about your accepting our *invitation*. (81 台北夜二專)

invoice 〔ˈɪnvɔɪs 〕 *n.* 發貨單；發票

The company included an *invoice* in the package that told me what goods were inside.

(88 保送甄試)

J j

journal 〔ˈdʒɝn! 〕 *n.* 期刊

My research paper was published in a famous *journal*. (78 四技工專)

justice 〔ˈdʒʌstɪs 〕 *n.* 正義

When people go to court they hope to find *justice*. (88 北區四技夜二專)

K k

kilometer (ˈkɪləˌmitɚ) *n.* 公里

Angela runs five *kilometers* every morning.

(86 保送甄試)

L l

labor (ˈlebɚ) *n.* 勞工

Labor insurance is one of the basic benefits
a company should offer to its emplyees.

(88 中區四技夜二專)

laborer (ˈlebərɚ) *n.* 勞工

In order to finish the construction project in
time we need to employ foreign *laborers*.

(84 台北夜二專)

language (ˈlæŋgwɪdʒ) *n.* 語言

English is so popular that it has already
become an international *language* used all
over the world. (77 師大工教)

length〔lɛŋθ〕 *n.* 長度

The street is three kilometers long. The *length* of the street is three kilometers.

（81 保送甄試）

letter〔'lɛtɚ〕 *n.* 字母

There are twenty-six *letters* in the English alphabet.（81 四技工專、師大工教）

liability〔ˌlaɪə'bɪlətɪ〕 *n.* 債務

A company may fail if it has more *liabilities* than assets.（81 台北夜二專）

library〔'laɪˌbrɛrɪ〕 *n.* 圖書館

A *library* has a collection of books.

（80 保送甄試）

limit〔'lɪmɪt〕 *n.* 限制

Through reading, one can gather information beyond the *limit* of time and space.（77 師大工教）

living (ˈlɪvɪŋ) *n.* 生計;生活

What does he do for a *living*? (90 科大、四技工專)

lobby (ˈlabɪ) *n.* 大廳

There are some public telephones in the hotel *lobby*. (89 科大、四技工專)

location (loˈkeʃən) *n.* 地點

This is a very good *location* for camping.

(77 四技商專)

log (lɔg) *n.* 原木

In the summer camp, we lived in a cabin built of *logs*. (83 北區夜二專)

M m

machinery (məˈʃɪnərɪ) *n.* 機器

Mechanical engineers are experts in *machinery*. (79 保送甄試)

magician (məˈdʒɪʃən) *n.* 魔術師

The *magician* performed his tricks with professional skill. (79 四技商專)

maintenance (ˈmentənəns) *n.* 維修；保養

The company needs someone with experience in the *maintenance* of computers.

(89科大、四技商、農專，88 南區四技夜二專)

major (ˈmedʒɚ) *n.* 主修科目

Mary's *major* at the university is mechanical engineering. (81 保送甄試)

management (ˈmænɪdʒmənt) *n.* 經營；管理

The store is under foreign *management*.

(81 保送甄試)

# 自我測驗

- [ ] interviewer   _____
- [ ] intruder   _____
- [ ] investigation   _____
- [ ] investment   _____
- [ ] invoice   _____

- [ ] journal   _____
- [ ] justice   _____
- [ ] labor   _____
- [ ] language   _____
- [ ] length   _____

- [ ] liability   _____
- [ ] lobby   _____
- [ ] log   _____
- [ ] machinery   _____
- [ ] maintenance   _____

 **Check List**

1. 入侵者　　i ___*intruder*___ r
2. 調　查　　i _____ n
3. 邀　請　　i _____ n
4. 發貨單　　i _____ e
5. 公　里　　k _____ r
6. 勞　工　　l _____ r
7. 語　言　　l _____ e
8. 字　母　　l _____ r
9. 圖書館　　l _____ y
10. 限　制　　l _____ t
11. 生　計　　l _____ g
12. 地　點　　l _____ n
13. 機　器　　m _____ y
14. 魔術師　　m _____ n
15. 主修科目　m _____ r

manufacturer 〔͵mænjəˈfæktʃərə 〕 *n.*
製造者；生產者
Hoping to increase business, the
manufacturers advertised their products
on the radio. (83 北區夜二專)

margin 〔ˈmɑrdʒɪn 〕 *n.* 頁邊空白
The teacher wrote some comments in the
margin of my paper. (89 科大、四技簡專、農科)

mask 〔 mæsk 〕 *n.* 面具；口罩
The thief wore a black *mask* so that no one
could recognize him. (83 保送甄試)

material 〔 məˈtɪrɪəl 〕 *n.* 原料；材料
Paper, bottles, and other useful *materials*
can be recycled. (89 北區四技夜二專)

maturity 〔 mə'tjʊrətɪ 〕 *n.* 成熟

This is the period during which the body attains *maturity*. (79 台北夜二專)

meaning 〔'minɪŋ 〕 *n.* 意義

Perhaps the most important use of a dictionary is to give the *meanings* of words.

(79 保送甄試)

measles 〔'mizḷz 〕 *n.* 麻疹

Measles is an infectious disease. (78 四技商專)

media 〔'midɪə 〕 *n. pl.* 媒體

Advertising messages are carried to large audiences by mass *media*. (80 彰化師大)

menu 〔'mɛnju 〕 *n.* 菜單

On special holidays, many restaurants serve set *menus*. (86 南區四技夜二專)

merchandise (ˋmɝtʃənˏdaɪz) n. 商品

The variety of *merchandise* in the store awed us. (78 師大工教)

message (ˋmɛsɪdʒ) n. 訊息

Will you take this *message* to my grandparents? (79 彰化師大)

metal (ˋmɛtḷ) n. 金屬

Iron is a kind of *metal*. (87 四技二專、彰師二教)

millimeter (ˋmɪləˏmitɚ) n. 公厘

The strong storm brought ten *millimeters* of rain. (86 保送甄試)

million (ˋmɪljən) n. 百萬

The *population* of Taipei is over two million.

(80 台北夜二專，81 保送甄試)

mine 〔maɪn〕 *n.* 寶庫

Peter is a *mine* of information. （78 台北夜二專）

mission 〔'mɪʃən〕 *n.* 任務；使命

It is the *mission* of this charity to help the poor. （89 四技二專）

modesty 〔'mɑdəstɪ〕 *n.* 謙虛

His *modesty* prevented him from taking any credit for the success. （87 四技商專、彰師商教）

moisture 〔'mɔɪstʃɚ〕 *n.* 水分；濕氣

The air in the desert is so dry that it contains hardly any *moisture*.

（86 四技商專、彰師商教）

moist	+	ture
潮濕的	+	*n.*

moment 〔'momənt〕 *n.* 瞬間；片刻

The *moment* the child was run down by a car, he was sent to a hospital. （77 師大工教）

monument 〔'mɑnjəmənt 〕 *n.* 紀念碑

The government will build a *monument* to
the soldiers. (89 科大、四技商專、農科)

muscle 〔'mʌsḷ 〕 *n.* 肌肉

John pulled a *muscle* in his leg while he
was playing basketball. (91 四技二專)

must 〔 mʌst 〕 *n.* 必要的事

All the factors involved being considered,
the construction of a new harbor in central
Taiwan is regarded as a *must*. (79 彰化師大)

N n

nation 〔'neʃən 〕 *n.* 國家

The *nations* of the world must work together
to conserve the world's resources, or life will
be very bad for our children. (83 四技商專、彰化師大)

neatness ﹝'nitnɪs﹞ *n.* 整潔

When my mother saw my room she praised me for my *neatness*. (89 技優保甄)

necessity ﹝ nə'sɛsətɪ﹞ *n.* 必需品

Food and clothing are *necessities* of life.

(83 保送甄試)

neck ﹝ nɛk ﹞ *n.* 脖子

Wear a scarf to protect your *neck* from the cold. (89 技優保甄)

needle ﹝'nidl̩﹞ *n.* 針;針頭

Drug users who inject drugs with a shared *needle* are particularly at risk. (89 技優保甄)

nerve ﹝ nɜv ﹞ *n.* 神經

The brain sends signals to the body through *nerves*. (89 技優保甄)

- ☐ margin   _____
- ☐ mask   _____
- ☐ maturity   _____
- ☐ measles   _____
- ☐ menu   _____

- ☐ merchandise   _____
- ☐ message   _____
- ☐ metal   _____
- ☐ millimeter   _____
- ☐ mine   _____

- ☐ moisture   _____
- ☐ muscle   _____
- ☐ must   _____
- ☐ neatness   _____
- ☐ neck   _____

Check List

1. 製造者   m <u>*manufacturer*</u> r
2. 原　料   m _____ l
3. 意　義   m _____ g
4. 媒　體   m _____ a
5. 商　品   m _____ e

6. 百　萬   m _____ n
7. 任　務   m _____ n
8. 謙　虛   m _____ y
9. 水　分   m _____ e
10. 瞬　間   m _____ t

11. 紀念碑   m _____ t
12. 國　家   n _____ n
13. 必需品   n _____ y
14. 針   n _____ e
15. 神　經   n _____ e

novel ('nɑvḷ) *n.* 小說

He has written two *novels*, but neither has been published yet. (89 技優保甄)

nurse (nɝs) *n.* 護士

If you cannot find the doctor, just ask the *nurse* to help you. (81 四技工專、師大工教)

nutrient ('njutrɪənt) *n.* 營養素

Young children need a lot of *nutrients* to help them grow. (80 四技商專，87 四技工專、師大工教)

nutrition (nju'trɪʃən) *n.* 營養

If you want to stay healthy, you need sufficient rest and proper *nutrition*.

(89 四技二專)

nutri	+ tion
|	|
nourish +	*n.*

O o

obedience 〔ə'bidɪəns〕 *n.* 服從

The commander demanded complete
obedience. (79 彰化師大)

obstacle 〔'ɑbstəkḷ〕 *n.* 障礙

The fallen tree was an *obstacle* to traffic.

(89 北區四技夜二專)

occasion 〔ə'keʒən〕 *n.* 場合;特殊的大事

Your graduation is an important *occasion*
for you and your family. (89 四技二專)

occupant 〔'ɑkjəpənt〕 *n.* 佔有者;居住者

Who is the *occupant* of the house?

(77 台北夜二專)

occupation 〔͵ɑkjə'peʃən 〕 *n.* 職業

If you confine your choice to a certain *occupation*, your chance of getting a job may become smaller. (80 四技商專)

Ocotber 〔 ɑk'tobə 〕 *n.* 十月

Our National Day is *October* the tenth.

(81 四技工專、師大工教)

opera 〔'ɑpərə 〕 *n.* 歌劇

Do you like to listen to Chinese *opera*?

(89 北區四技夜二專)

opportunity 〔͵ɑpə'tjunətɪ 〕 *n.* 機會

Traveling abroad will give you the *opportunity* to learn about other cultures.

(90 科大、四技工專)

opposite 〔'ɑpəzɪt 〕 *n.* 相反的 (人、事、字)

What is the *opposite* of "industrious"?

(88 四技二專)

optimism 〔'ɑptə,mɪzəm 〕 *n.* 樂觀

Optimism, which means hoping for the best, is much better than pessimism.

（83 四技商專、彰化師大）

outcome 〔'aʊt,kʌm 〕 *n.* 結果

The *outcome* of the election was announced two weeks ago. （86 中區四技夜二專）

outline 〔'aʊt,laɪn 〕 *n.* 大綱；概要

It is a good idea to prepare an *outline* before you write your paper. （88 保送甄試）

output 〔'aʊt,pʊt 〕 *n.* 產量

Some companies build new machinery and tools to increase their total *output*.

（88 保送甄試）

P p

package ﹙'pækɪdʒ﹚ *n.* 包裹

I must take this *package* to the post office.

（91 四技二專）

page ﹙ pedʒ ﹚ *n.* 頁

You can find the explanation on *page* 63.

（77 四技工專）

parliament ﹙'pɑrləmənt ﹚ *n.* 國會

The prime minister will speak to both houses of *parliament* this afternoon. （86 保送甄試）

partnership ﹙'pɑrtnɚˌʃɪp ﹚ *n.* 合夥關係

Have you ever considered entering into *partnership* with him? （87 四技商專、彰師商教）

passenger ﹙'pæsn̩dʒɚ ﹚ *n.* 乘客

It was easy to find seats on the train because there were so few *passengers*. （83 四技工專、師大工教）

passport (ˈpæsˌport) *n.* 護照

When you cross the border of a country,
you usually have to show your *passport*.

(81 保送甄試)

patient (ˈpeʃənt) *n.* 病人

No sooner had the accident happened than
the ambulance took the *patients* to the
hospital. (86 四技商專、彰師商教)

pedestrian (pəˈdɛstrɪən) *n.* 行人

A good driver watches out for *pedestrians*
that are crossing the road.

(89 科大、四技工專)

pedestr	+ ian
foot	+ 人

penalty (ˈpɛnḷtɪ) *n.* 刑罰

The *penalty* for robbery is death. There can
be no exception to the law. (81 保送甄試)

- [ ] novel   _____
- [ ] nurse   _____
- [ ] nutrition   _____
- [ ] occasion   _____
- [ ] occupant   _____

- [ ] October   _____
- [ ] opera   _____
- [ ] opposite   _____
- [ ] outcome   _____
- [ ] output   _____

- [ ] package   _____
- [ ] painstaking   _____
- [ ] parliament   _____
- [ ] passenger   _____
- [ ] patient   _____

Check List

1. 小　說　　　n ___*novel*___ l
2. 營養素　　　n _____ t
3. 服　從　　　o _____ e
4. 障　礙　　　o _____ e
5. 場　合　　　o _____ n
6. 佔有者　　　o _____ t
7. 職　業　　　o _____ n
8. 機　會　　　o _____ y
9. 樂　觀　　　o _____ m
10. 結　果　　　o _____ e
11. 大　綱　　　o _____ e
12. 合夥關係　　p _____ p
13. 乘　客　　　p _____ r
14. 護　照　　　p _____ t
15. 行　人　　　p _____ n

percent〔pɚˈsɛnt〕*n.* 百分比

Twenty is twenty *percent* of one hundred.

（81 保送甄試）

performance〔pɚˈfɔrməns〕*n.* 表演

The musician gave a wonderful *performance* at the concert hall.（90 科大、四技工專）

period〔ˈpɪrɪəd〕*n.* 時期

Before Ang Lee's films started to attract international attention, he had been out of work for a *period* of time.（90 科大、四技二專）

permission〔pɚˈmɪʃən〕*n.* 許可

Without special *permission*, no one can visit the castle.（80 師大工教）

per	+ miss	+ ion
|	|	|
through	+ *send*	+ *n.* （通過每一關）

perseverance 〔͵pɝsəˈvɪrəns 〕 *n.* 毅力

Both patience and *perseverance* are
necessary if one expects to succeed in life.

（79 四技商專）

person 〔ˈpɝsn̩ 〕 *n.* 人

"VIP"means Very Important *Person*.

（88 南區四技夜二專）

pet 〔 pɛt 〕 *n.* 寵物

Animals that you like very much and keep
at home are *pets*. （86 南區四技夜二專）

petroleum 〔 pəˈtrolɪəm 〕 *n.* 石油

Petroleum is used to produce gasoline.

（89 北區四技夜二專）

petr	+ oleum
rock	+ *oil*

pilot 〔ˈpaɪlət 〕 *n.* 飛行員

The *pilot* announced that we would be
landing in Taipei shortly. （79 北區夜二專）

planet (ˈplænɪt) *n.* 行星

Venus is one of the *planets* moving around the sun. (89科大、四技工專)

plant (plænt) *n.* 植物

Roses, water lilies, chrysanthemums, etc. are garden *plants*. (88 中區四技夜二專)

pollution (pəˈluʃən) *n.* 污染

Air *pollution* is very serious in many large cities. (78 四技工專)

population (ˌpɑpjəˈleʃən) *n.* 人口

The *population* of Taiwan was calculated roughly at 22,000,000.

(80 台北夜二專，81 保送甄試，88 中區四技夜二專)

post (post) *n.* 職位

He resigned from the *post* of president last week. (81 台北夜二專)

postage (ˈpostɪdʒ) *n.* 郵資

Our government has decided
to raise the *postage* on July
20th. (80 四技商專)

post + age
| |
郵件 + *n.*

poverty (ˈpɑvətɪ) *n.* 貧窮

There are still many people living in a state
of *poverty* in the world today.

(82 四技商專、彰化師大)

prediction (prɪˈdɪkʃən) *n.* 預測

Do you believe in the *predictions* made by
fortunetellers? (89 中區夜四技二專)

premium (ˈprimɪəm) *n.* 優惠

The storeowner offered me a *premium* —
buy one, get one free. (89 北區四技夜二專)

present (ˈprɛznt) *n.* 禮物

Richard's birthday is on Tuesday; we should buy a *present* for him. (83 四技工專、師大工教)

presentation (ˌprɛzɛnˈteʃən) *n.* 描述

A well-written *presentation* can create a strong impression that will help you a lot in getting a good job. (89 中區夜四技二專)

preservation (ˌprɛzɚˈveʃən) *n.* 保存；維持

Exercise, fresh air and sleep are essential for the *preservation* of health.

(82 四技工專、師大工教)

```
pre  + serv + ation
 |      |      |
before + keep +  n. ( 保存在之前的狀態 )
```

pressure (ˈprɛʃɚ) *n.* 壓力

People who are fat or overweight often have high blood *pressure*. (81 保送甄試)

principal ('prɪnsəpḷ) *n.* 本金

The borrower must return the *principal*,
which is the money that was borrowed,
plus the interest. (81 四技商專，83 四技商專、彰化師大)

prison ('prɪzn̩) *n.* 監獄

The man, having committed lots of crimes,
was finally arrested and put into *prison*.

(86 保送甄試)

probability (prɑbə'bɪlətɪ) *n.* 可能性

According to the weather report, there is a
high *probability* of rain this afternoon.

(89 科大、四技商專、農科)

program ('progræm) *n.* 節目

There are *programs* on television that
explain how to do things. (80 保送甄試)

自我測驗

- [ ] performance _____
- [ ] period _____
- [ ] person _____
- [ ] pet _____
- [ ] pilot _____

- [ ] planet _____
- [ ] plant _____
- [ ] pollution _____
- [ ] post _____
- [ ] postage _____

- [ ] poverty _____
- [ ] premium _____
- [ ] preservation _____
- [ ] principal _____
- [ ] prison _____

 **Check List**

1. 百分比　　p ___*percent*___ t
2. 表　演　　p _____ e
3. 許　可　　p _____ n
4. 毅　力　　p _____ e
5. 石　油　　p _____ m

6. 行　星　　p _____ t
7. 人　口　　p _____ n
8. 郵　資　　p _____ e
9. 預　測　　p _____ n
10. 禮　物　　p _____ t

11. 描　述　　p _____ n
12. 壓　力　　p _____ e
13. 本　金　　p _____ l
14. 可能性　　p _____ y
15. 節　目　　p _____ m

progress (ˈprɑɡrɛs) *n.* 進步

David has made great *progress* in math.

（89 科大、四技工專）

prohibition (ˌproəˈbɪʃən) *n.* 禁止

For the good of the students' health, the *prohibition* against smoking on school campus should be strictly enforced.

（84 四技商專、彰師商教）

project (ˈprɑdʒɛkt) *n.* 計劃；企劃

We will have to finish the class *project* by the end of the semester.（89 四技二專）

promotion (prəˈmoʃən) *n.* 升遷；晉級

There are good prospects of advancement; therefore, *promotion* will depend entirely on your own ability and industry. （77 四技商專）

property (ˈprɑpətɪ) *n.* 特性

Important *properties* of matter include mass, taste, smell, etc. (84 保送甄試)

purchase (ˈpɝtʃəs) *n.* 購買

The house owner will lower the price of the house if the Lins agree to make a *purchase* in two weeks. (84 四技商專、彰師商教，90 科大、四技二專)

purpose (ˈpɝpəs) *n.* 目的

The *purpose* of the contest is to give students a chance to show off their talents.

(88 科大、四技工專)

Q q

quarter (ˈkwɔrtə) *n.* (比賽的) 一節

John will play in the second *quarter* of the game. (81 台北夜二專)

R r

rail〔 rel 〕 *n.* 鐵軌

A train runs on *rails*. (80 保送甄試)

railroad 〔ˈrelˌrod 〕 *n.* 鐵路

The Republic of China has many good *railroads* and highways used for transportation. (78 四技簡專)

rainfall 〔ˈrenˌfɔl 〕 *n.* 降雨

Since there is almost no *rainfall*, the farmers can't have good harvests. (88 保送甄試)

rash 〔 ræʃ 〕 *n.* 疹子

Some people are allergic to seafood and they'll develop a *rash* and itch all over after eating it. (86 保送甄試)

reality 〔 rɪˈælətɪ 〕 *n.* 真實；現實

She gives the impression of being generous, but in *reality* she is a very selfish woman.

（83 保送甄試）

receipt 〔 rɪˈsit 〕 *n.* 收據

Don't forget to ask the store for a *receipt* when you buy something. （87 台北夜二專）

receptacle 〔 rɪˈsɛptəkḷ 〕 *n.* 容器；儲藏所

A *receptacle* is a container that can hold liquids or solids. （89 技優保甄）

reception 〔 rɪˈsɛpʃən 〕 *n.* 接待；歡迎

I was given a warm *reception* when I first joined the company. （78 四技商專，86 中區四技夜二專）

receptionist 〔 rɪˈsɛpʃənɪst 〕 *n.* 接待員

Sometimes a medical secretary working for a doctor also acts as a *receptionist*. （79 彰化師大）

recession 〔 rɪ'sɛʃən 〕 *n.* 不景氣

Because *recession* was forecast, many investors sold their shares of stock.

（83 北區夜二專）

re	+ cess	+ ion
back +	*go* +	*n.* （經濟向後退）

recipe 〔'rɛsəpɪ 〕 *n.* 食譜

This is my grandmother's *recipe* for apple pie. （79 北區夜二專）

recommendation 〔 ˌrɛkəmɛn'deʃən 〕 *n.* 推薦

I didn't know what to order, so I asked the waiter for a *recommendation*. （89 北區四技夜二專）

reduction 〔 rɪ'dʌkʃən 〕 *n.* （價格的）折扣

They made a *reduction* of 10% in the price of the camera. （80 彰化師大）

refrigerator 〔rɪˈfrɪdʒəˌretə 〕 *n.* 冰箱

My sister-in-law usually goes shopping once a week, and during the week she depends upon her *refrigerator* to keep the food fresh.

（79 四技工專，83 北區夜二專，86 四技商專、彰師商教）

refund 〔ˈriˌfʌnd 〕 *n.* 退錢

Melvin took the clothing back to the store and tried to get a *refund* but they refused to give him his money back.

（85 四技商專、彰化師大，86 台北夜二專）

regards 〔rɪˈgɑrdz 〕 *n. pl.* 問候

We send our kindest *regards* and look forward to hearing from you.

（85 四技商專、彰化師大，82 嘉南、高屏區夜二專）

regulation 〔ˌrɛgjəˈleʃən 〕 *n.* 規定

It's against the *regulations* to park your car here. （89 北區四技夜二專）

 自我測驗

- [ ] progress　　_____
- [ ] project　　_____
- [ ] property　　_____
- [ ] purpose　　_____
- [ ] quarter　　_____

- [ ] rail　　_____
- [ ] rash　　_____
- [ ] receipt　　_____
- [ ] receptable　　_____
- [ ] receptionist　　_____

- [ ] recipe　　_____
- [ ] reduction　　_____
- [ ] refrigerator　　_____
- [ ] refund　　_____
- [ ] regards　　_____

1. 進　步　　p ___*progress*___ s
2. 禁　止　　p _____ n
3. 升　遷　　p _____ n
4. 購　買　　p _____ e
5. 鐵　路　　r _____ d

6. 降　雨　　r _____ l
7. 發　疹　　r _____ h
8. 眞　實　　r _____ y
9. 收　據　　r _____ t
10. 接　待　　r _____ n

11. 不景氣　　r _____ n
12. 推　薦　　r _____ n
13. 折　扣　　r _____ n
14. 退　錢　　r _____ d
15. 規　定　　r _____ n

relationship ﹝ rɪ'leʃənˌʃɪp ﹞ *n.* 關係

If gift-giving is done properly, it can help
you build good personal *relationships*.

（85 四技商專、彰化師大）

relative ﹝'rɛlətɪv ﹞ *n.* 親戚

My grandmother is the *relative* I like to visit
most. （89 技優保甄）

relief ﹝ rɪ'lif ﹞ *n.* 解除；放鬆

It was a great *relief* to learn that his son was
safe. （81 台北夜二專）

religion ﹝ rɪ'lɪdʒən ﹞ *n.* 宗教

Christianity is a popular *religion* in the
Western world. （89 四技二專，89 科大、四技商、農專）

reminder 〔 rɪ'maɪndə 〕 *n.* 提醒的人或物

Every photo is a *reminder* of a very beautiful day. (89 四技二專)

re	+ mind +	er
|	|	|
against +	心 +	人或物

request 〔 rɪ'kwɛst 〕 *n.* 要求

We made a *request* to them for the information. (89 四技二專)

requirement 〔 rɪ'kwaɪrmənt 〕 *n.* 必要條件

Concentration is the first *requirement* for learning. (88 北區四技夜二專)

rescue 〔'rɛskju 〕 *n.* 拯救

You can escape or increase your chances of *rescue* if you use your head and know what to do in a big fire. (82 四技商專、彰化師大)

residence ('rɛzədəns) *n.* 住所

The maid answered the phone by saying, "This is the mayor's *residence*." (79 台北夜二專)

resources (rɪ'sorsɪz) *n. pl.* 資源

America is rich in natural *resources*, such as iron, oil, and so forth. (83 保送甄試，87 台北夜二專)

respect (rɪ'spɛkt) *n.* 方面

Business letters differ from personal letters in many *respects*. (87 中區四技夜二專)

responsibility (rɪ,spɑnsə'bɪlətɪ) *n.* 責任

John had to assume the *responsibility* of educating his brother's children. (79 彰化師大)

resume (,rɛzju'me) *n.* 履歷表

In most cases, job candidates will also send prospective employers a *resume*. (82 北區夜二專)

revenue (ˈrɛvəˌnju) *n.* 稅收

A country's *revenue* comes mostly from taxes. (79 四技商專)

```
re   + venue
 |      |
back + come ( 回到政府的錢 )
```

revolution (ˌrɛvəˈluʃən) *n.* 革命

He knows the names of all the heroes of the American *Revolution*. (89 中區夜四技二專)

risk (rɪsk) *n.* 危險

Businessmen recognize the convenience of being protected from running certain *risks*.

(80 台中夜二專)

robot (ˈrobət) *n.* 機器人

A *robot,* which acts like a man, can do the same work without getting bored. (80 台北夜二專)

rule 〔 rul 〕 *n.* 規則

Traffic *rules* should be observed by anyone using the road. (85 保送甄試)

S s

salary 〔'sælərɪ 〕 *n.* 薪水

It's a new job with a good *salary*. But it's dangerous work. Should I take it? (89 技優保甄)

salesman 〔'selzmən 〕 *n.* 售貨員

The *salesman* told me those shirts were sold out but that they might be available again two weeks later. (86 保送甄試)

sample 〔'sæmpl 〕 *n.* 樣品

The clerk gave me a *sample* of the mango ice cream, and it was so good that I decided to buy some. (89 技優保甄)

satellite ('sætḷ,aɪt) *n.* 衛星

The new *satellite* will carry messages from all over the world. (89 技優保甄)

satisfaction (,sætɪs'fækʃən) *n.* 滿意

Nothing can compare with the sense of *satisfaction* you will feel when you complete the work. (90 科大、四技工專)

savings ('sevɪŋz) *n. pl.* 儲蓄

They deposit money in a *savings* account at the bank. (78 四技商專)

scholar ('skɑlɚ) *n.* 學者

He is a *scholar* of ancient history.

(89 北區四技夜二專)

scribble ('skrɪbḷ) *n.* 塗鴉；亂寫

The kid didn't write his name, but just made a *scribble* on the board. (85 四技商專、彰化師大)

 自我測驗

☐ relationship   _____

☐ relief   _____

☐ religion   _____

☐ reminder   _____

☐ requirement   _____

☐ rescue   _____

☐ resources   _____

☐ resume   _____

☐ revolution   _____

☐ risk   _____

☐ rule   _____

☐ sample   _____

☐ statellite   _____

☐ savings   _____

☐ scholar   _____

Check List

1. 親　戚　　r ___*relative*___ e
2. 要　求　　r _____ t
3. 拯　救　　r _____ e
4. 住　所　　r _____ e
5. 方　面　　r _____ t

6. 責　任　　r _____ y
7. 履歷表　　r _____ e
8. 稅　收　　r _____ e
9. 革　命　　r _____ n
10. 機器人　　r _____ t

11. 薪　水　　s _____ y
12. 售貨員　　s _____ n
13. 衛　星　　s _____ e
14. 滿　意　　s _____ n
15. 塗　鴉　　s _____ e

secretary ('sɛkrə,tɛrɪ) *n.* 秘書

Jessica works in a big company as a *secretary*, and often uses a typewriter and a computer to do her work.

（79 彰化師大，83 四技工專、師大工教）

sequence ('sikwəns) *n.* 連續

The passengers were asked to board the plane in *sequence*, according to their seat numbers. （88 北區四技夜二專）

series ('sirɪz) *n.* 影集；系列

One episode of this television *series* is shown every night. （87 保送甄試）

service ('sɝvɪs) *n.* 服務

I don't understand why people put up with the bad *service* in this restaurant. （79 師大工教）

sewage 〔'sjuɪdʒ 〕 *n.* 污水

Sewage is waste water from houses, restaurants, office buildings and factories.

（84 台北夜二專）

shame 〔 ʃem 〕 *n.* 羞恥；慚愧

There is no *shame* in making mistakes.

（89 技優保甄）

sheep 〔 ʃip 〕 *n.* 綿羊

Most of the *sheep* raised for their wool are of a breed named Merino. （83 四技商專、彰化師大）

shelter 〔'ʃɛltɚ 〕 *n.* 庇護所；避難所

The original meaning of home is the best *shelter* where one can go for help. （88 四技商專）

shift 〔 ʃɪft 〕 *n.* 輪班

Since he is working on the night *shift*, he has to be on duty from 10 p.m. to 6 a.m.

（84 保送甄試）

shock ﹝ ʃɑk ﹞ *n.* 電擊

A worn-out cord can cause an electric *shock* or start a fire. (84 保送甄試)

shower ﹝'ʃaʊɚ ﹞ *n.* 淋浴

Everyone is required to take a *shower* before entering the swimming pool. (90 科大、四技工專)

sign ﹝ saɪ ﹞ *n.* 標誌；告示

The *sign* says that swimming is not allowed here. (87 四技商專、彰師商敎)

signal ﹝'sɪgn̩ ﹞ *n.* 信號

The referee gave the *signal* to start the game.

(89 四技二專)

software ﹝'sɔft͵wɛr ﹞ *n.* 軟體

It took the *software* company one month to figure out how to fight the PC virus, which attacks personal computers through e-mails.

(90 科大、四技二專)

soil 〔 sɔɪl 〕 *n.* 土壤

Plants need sun, water, and good *soil*.

（81 保送甄試）

stair 〔 stɛr 〕 *n.* 樓梯

The elevator is not working. We'll have to
take the *stairs*. （89 四技二專）

standard 〔'stændəd 〕 *n.* 水準

The *standard* of living in many countries in
the world has been greatly improved.

（82 保送甄試）

statement 〔'stetmənt 〕 *n.* 陳述

The politician was asked to make a *statement*
to the reporters. （89 四技二專）

```
state  + ment
  |        |
stand +  n. ( 站著說話 )
```

stationery (ˈsteʃənˌɛrɪ) *n.* 文具

Stationery is writing materials such as pens, pencils, and paper. (86 四技商專、彰師商教)

statue (ˈstætʃʊ) *n.* 雕像

There is a *statue* of the famous poet in the park. (86 保送甄試)

step (stɛp) *n.* 步驟

This flow chart shows all the *steps* that are necessary to do this job. (80 保送甄試)

storage (ˈstɔrɪdʒ) *n.* 貯藏

We keep the things that we don't use very often in the *storage* room. (86 保送甄試)

stove (stov) *n.* 爐子

I was not able to cook because the *stove* was broken. (89 北區四技夜二專)

starvation 〔 stɑr'veʃən 〕 *n.* 餓死

People in Ethiopia are under the threat of *starvation* because of the long dry seasons and unstable political situation. (80 四技工專)

stream 〔 strim 〕 *n.* 小溪

You need to cross a deep *stream* before you reach the cottage. (87 中區四技夜二專)

strength 〔 strɛŋθ 〕 *n.* 優點

It is important for people to accept their weaknesses as well as their *strengths*.

(80 彰化師大)

stress 〔 strɛs 〕 *n.* 壓力

Nowadays, many people live under *stress*.

(85 台北夜二專)

stretcher 〔'strɛtʃɚ 〕 *n.* 擔架

The firemen carried the injured man on a *stretcher*. (87 四技工專、師大工教)

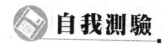 **自我測驗**

- ☐ secretary _____
- ☐ series _____
- ☐ service _____
- ☐ shame _____
- ☐ sheep _____

- ☐ shock _____
- ☐ shower _____
- ☐ sign _____
- ☐ software _____
- ☐ soil _____

- ☐ stair _____
- ☐ stationery _____
- ☐ step _____
- ☐ stove _____
- ☐ stream _____

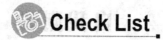

1. 連　續　　s ___sequence___ e
2. 污　水　　s _____ e
3. 羞　恥　　s _____ e
4. 庇護所　　s _____ r
5. 輪　班　　s _____ t

6. 信　號　　s _____ l
7. 軟　體　　s _____ e
8. 水　準　　s _____ d
9. 陳　述　　s _____ t
10. 雕　像　　s _____ e

11. 貯　藏　　s _____ e
12. 餓　死　　s _____ n
13. 優　點　　s _____ h
14. 壓　力　　s _____ s
15. 擔　架　　s _____ r

structure ('strʌktʃɚ) *n.* 建築物

The Shin Kong tower is one of the largest *structures* in the city. (89科大、四技工專)

struggle ('strʌgl̩) *n.* 奮鬥；競爭

The *struggle* for survival is very severe in nature. (80保送甄試)

subway ('sʌb,we) *n.* 地下鐵

The *subway* is one of the most convenient means of transportation. (88北區四技夜二專)

success (sək'sɛs) *n.* 成功

Paul's *success* in business is due to his friend's help. (89科大、四技工專)

suggestion (sə'dʒɛstʃən) *n.* 建議

When planning the party, our class leader asked us for *suggestions*. (89四技二專)

superstition 〔͵supɚˈstɪʃən 〕 *n.* 迷信

There is a *superstition* that if you break a mirror, you'll have bad luck for seven years.

（83 保送甄試）

supervisor 〔͵supɚˈvaɪzɚ 〕 *n.* 監督者；
管理人

The *supervisor* was responsible for explaining the new regulations to the workers. （91 四技二專）

supper 〔ˈsʌpɚ 〕 *n.* 晚餐

John had *supper* with his friends at a fast-food restaurant. （89 科大、四技工專）

supply 〔səˈplaɪ 〕 *n.* 供給；供應

The *supply* of food in Africa can not keep up with the demand. （88 科大、四技工專）

support 〔 sə'port 〕 *n.* 支持

I would never have won the election without your *support*. (91 四技二專)

surface 〔 'sɝfɪs 〕 *n.* 表面

About three-fourths of the earth's *surface* is covered by water. (79 保送甄試)

survival 〔 sə'vaɪv! 〕 *n.* 存活；生還

Hopes are fading for the *survival* of the missing mountain climbers. (84 四技商專、彰師商教)

suspense 〔 sə'spɛns 〕 *n.* 焦慮；懸疑

Tell me what happened to him. Don't keep me in *suspense*. (86 中區四技夜二專)

sweeping 〔 'swipɪŋ 〕 *n.* 掃地

Housekeeping involves cooking, washing dishes, *sweeping*, and cleaning. (83 保送甄試)

switch 〔 swɪtʃ 〕 *n.* 開關

I want to turn on the light. Where is the *switch*? (77 四技工專)

symbol 〔 'sɪmbḷ 〕 *n.* 象徵

The dove is a *symbol* of peace. (79 保送甄試)

symptom 〔 'sɪmptəm 〕 *n.* 症狀

Symptoms of AIDS may not show up until a few years after a person is infected.

(87 四技工專、師大工教)

```
  sym    + ptom
   |        |
together + fall ( 和疾病一起降臨 )
```

synonym 〔 'sɪnə,nɪm 〕 *n.* 同義字

"Motorcar" and "automobile" are *synonyms*.

(80 台北夜二專)

system ('sɪstəm) *n.* 系統

A good transportation *system* is essential to the development of an industrial nation.

（77 四技商專）

T t

target ('tɑrgɪt) *n.* 目標

Although he had never used a bow and arrow before, he was able to hit the *target*.

（89 科大、四技工專）

telephone ('tɛlə,fon) *n.* 電話

Now people almost everywhere in the world can speak to each other by *telephone*.

（77 四技工專）

telescope ('tɛlə,skop) *n.* 望遠鏡

If you want to look at stars more clearly, you have to use a *telescope*. （78 四技工專）

temper (ˈtɛmpɚ) *n.* 脾氣

It is a kind of virtue to keep one's *temper*.

（86 四技商專、彰師商教）

temperature (ˈtɛmpərətʃɚ) *n.* 體溫

The nurse took my *temperature* and told me I had a fever. （82 四技商專、彰化師大，84 四技商專、彰師商教）

terminal (ˈtɝmənļ) *n.* 航空站

The new airport has two *terminals*.

（89 北區四技夜二專）

thermometer (θəˈmɑmətɚ) *n.* 溫度計

Mrs. Chang took the temperature of her daughter with a *thermometer*. （87 四技工專、師大工教）

toast (tost) *n.* 敬酒

In a Chinese restaurant, we can often hear people say "Bottoms up!" when they make *toasts* with wine. （89 四技二專）

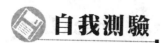# 自我測驗

- ☐ subway _____
- ☐ success _____
- ☐ suggestion _____
- ☐ supper _____
- ☐ supply _____

- ☐ support _____
- ☐ surface _____
- ☐ sweeping _____
- ☐ switch _____
- ☐ symbol _____

- ☐ system _____
- ☐ telephone _____
- ☐ temper _____
- ☐ terminal _____
- ☐ toast _____

 **Check List**

1. 建築物　　s _structure_ e
2. 奮　鬥　　s _____ e
3. 迷　信　　s _____ n
4. 監督者　　s _____ r
5. 存　活　　s _____ l

6. 焦　慮　　s _____ e
7. 症　狀　　s _____ m
8. 同義字　　s _____ m
9. 系　統　　s _____ m
10. 目　標　　t _____ t

11. 望遠鏡　　t _____ e
12. 脾　氣　　t _____ r
13. 體　溫　　t _____ e
14. 溫度計　　t _____ r
15. 敬　酒　　t _____ t

tool〔tul〕 *n.* 工具

A telephone is a very useful *tool* for communication.（80 保送甄試）

trade〔tred〕 *n.* 貿易

Before starting the business, we need a *trade* agreement.（79 四技商專）

traffic〔'træfɪk〕 *n.* 交通

Traffic will improve when the city has a mass rapid transit system.（89 技優保甄）

trainer〔'trenɚ〕 *n.* 訓練者

The dog *trainer* was able to teach the dog many tricks.（89 技優保甄）

transaction〔træns'ækʃən〕 *n.* 交易

Transactions happen all over the world as international trade becomes more and more important.（80 台中夜二專）

transcript (ˈtrænˌskrɪpt) *n.* (根據錄音的)
文字紀錄

After listening to the tape, you should read
the *transcript* of the conversation. (88四技二專)

translation (trænsˈleʃən) *n.* 翻譯本

This book is a French *translation* of the first
Harry Potter book. (89技優保甄)

trans	+	la	+ tion
across	+	*bring*	+ *n.* (移向別處)

transportation (ˌtrænspɚˈteʃən) *n.*
運輸；交通工具

I usually go to work by taking a bus as my
transportation. (80、81台北夜二專，88四技商專、北區四
技夜二專，89技優保甄)

trash (træʃ) *n.* 垃圾

We should take the *trash* out before nine
o'clock. (89技優保甄)

treatment (ˈtritmənt) *n.* 治療

The wounded are taken to the hospital for *treatment*. (77 四技工專)

trial (ˈtraɪəl) *n.* 審判

Sometimes the company sends a famous lawyer to attend a *trial* to help prisoners.

(81 保送甄試)

trunk (trʌŋk) *n.* 行李箱

They packed the *trunk* of the car with food.

(82 北區夜二專)

turnover (ˈtɜnˌovɚ) *n.* (商品的) 流動率

A food market that is busy and has a quick *turnover* will assure you of fresher food.

(84 保送甄試)

twins (twɪnz) *n. pl.* 雙胞胎

The *twins* were so much alike that it was difficult for us to distinguish one from the other. (86 中區四技夜二專)

typhoon〔taɪˈfun〕*n.* 颱風

The train was delayed by the *typhoon*.

(79 彰化師大)

V v

vacationland〔veˈkeʃənˌlænd〕*n.*
度假勝地

Taiwan still has a long way to go to catch
up with well-known *vacationlands* as
Switzerland and Spain. (77 四技商專)

vaccine〔ˈvæksin〕*n.* 疫苗

The scientists hope to develop a *vaccine*
that will prevent the common cold.

(87 四技工專、師大工教)

value〔ˈvælju〕*n.* 價值

This book will be of great *value* to students
of history. (82 保送甄試)

vapor (ˈvepɚ) *n.* 蒸氣

The boiling water produced a thick *vapor*.

(86 四技商專、彰師商教)

variety (vəˈraɪətɪ) *n.* 變化

Mary's life is full of *variety*.

(78 師大工教，86 中區四技夜二專，88 中區四技夜二專)

vegetable (ˈvɛdʒətəbḷ) *n.* 蔬菜

It is difficult to grow good *vegetables* in the poor soil in this area. (79 師大工教)

vehicle (ˈviɪkḷ) *n.* 車輛

Gasoline is used as a fuel for cars, trucks and other *vehicles*. (83 保送甄試)

vessel (ˈvɛsḷ) *n.* 船

You can always see many *vessels* in the busy harbor. (82 四技工專、師大工教，87 四技工專、師大工教)

vibration 〔 vaɪˈbreʃən 〕 *n.* 震動

When the rocket was launched, the spectators could feel a *vibration* in the ground. (87 四技商專、彰師商教)

vitamin 〔ˈvaɪtəmɪn 〕 *n.* 維他命

One of the most effective ways to stay healthy is to eat foods that are rich in *vitamins*. (79 保送甄試)

```
vit  + tamin
 |       |
live +   n. ( 維持生命的物質 )
```

voice 〔 vɔɪs 〕 *n.* 聲音

Please lower your *voice*. This is a library.

(89 四技二專)

 **自我測驗**

- [ ] tool   _____
- [ ] trade   _____
- [ ] traffic   _____
- [ ] transcript   _____
- [ ] trash   _____

- [ ] trunk   _____
- [ ] turnover   _____
- [ ] twins   _____
- [ ] typhoon   _____
- [ ] value   _____

- [ ] vapor   _____
- [ ] vegetable   _____
- [ ] vehicle   _____
- [ ] vitamin   _____
- [ ] voice   _____

Check List

1. 貿　易　　t _____*trade*_____ e
2. 交　易　　t _____ n
3. 文字紀錄　t _____ t
4. 訓練者　　t _____ r
5. 運　輸　　t _____ n

6. 治　療　　t _____ t
7. 審　判　　t _____ l
8. 雙胞胎　　t _____ s
9. 渡假勝地　v _____ d
10. 疫　苗　　v _____ e

11. 蒸　氣　　v _____ r
12. 變　化　　v _____ y
13. 船　　　　v _____ l
14. 震　動　　v _____ n
15. 維他命　　v _____ n

W w

warrant 〔'wɔrənt 〕 *n.* （法院的）令狀
Our houses cannot be searched without a
search *warrant.* (85 四技商專、彰化師大)

weapon 〔'wɛpən 〕 *n.* 武器
Swords, arrows, guns, claws, horns, and
teeth are *weapons.* (83 保送甄試)

wedding 〔'wɛdɪŋ 〕 *n.* 婚禮
Mary will get married next week.　Are you
going to her *wedding*? (86 四技工專、師大工教)

Wednesday 〔'wɛnzdɪ 〕 *n.* 星期三
The day between Tuesday and Thursday
is *Wednesday.* (77 師大工教)

whistle〔'hwɪsḷ〕 *n.* 哨子

The police officer blew his *whistle* to signal the cars to stop. (89技優保甄)

worship〔'wɝʃɪp〕 *n.* 禮拜

Most Christians go to church on Sunday to attend *worship*. (89科大、四技簡專、農科)

Y y

yogurt〔'jogɚt〕 *n.* 優格

Milk is not the only dairy product you can eat, you also can choose ice cream, *yogurt*, and cheese. (86南區四技夜二專)

youth〔juθ〕 *n.* 年輕

He has all the appearance of *youth*.

(82四技工專、師大工教)

動 詞

accept 〔 ək'sɛpt 〕 v. 接受

He dislikes Peter; he would not *accept* his offer. (82 四技工專、師大工教，81 台北夜二專)

accompany 〔 ə'kʌmpənɪ 〕 v. 伴隨

The rain was *accompanied* by a strong wind.

(89 中區夜四技二專)

accumulate 〔 ə'kjumjə,let 〕 v. 累積

It is snowing so hard that three inches have *accumulated* since this morning. (87 保送甄試)

```
ac  +  cumulate
|        |
to  +  heap up ( 累積 )
```

achieve 〔 ə'tʃiv 〕 v. 達到

As soon as you *achieve* one goal, set another one. (91 四技二專)

acquaint ﹝ ə'kwent ﹞ v. 使認識

They have been *acquainted* with each other for a long time. (79 四技商專)

acquire ﹝ ə'kwaɪr ﹞ v. 獲得;養成

A bad habit, once *acquired*, can't be gotten rid of easily.

(87 保送甄試,89 科大、四技工專)

```
ac + quire
 |      |
to + seek
```

adjust ﹝ ə'dʒʌst ﹞ v. 使適應

We *adjusted* ourselves to the hot weather.

(79 四技商專)

admire ﹝ əd'maɪr ﹞ v. 欣賞

She looked into the mirror and *admired* her own beauty. (89 中區夜四技二專)

admit ﹝ əd'mɪt ﹞ v. 承認

He refused to *admit* that he had cheated on the test. (91 四技二專)

advance ﹝əd'væns﹞ *v.* 前進；晉升

A worker can *advance* to a better position if he works hard. (86 台北夜二專)

affect ﹝ə'fɛkt﹞ *v.* 影響

Events of earliest childhood often profoundly *affect* one's later life. (82 四技工專、師大工教)

afford ﹝ə'ford，ə'fɔrd﹞ *v.* 負擔得起

This is not expensive, so I can *afford* to buy it.

(86 南區四技夜二專，83 保送甄試)

agree ﹝ə'gri﹞ *v.* 同意

Gao Xingjian, who won the Nobel Prize for literature in 2000, has *agreed* to teach in eastern Taiwan this summer. (90 科大、四技二專)

aim ﹝em﹞ *v.* 打算

The owner of the goods *aims* first at protecting himself against losses. (78 四技商專)

alarm〔ə'lɑrm〕v. 使驚慌

We were *alarmed* by the loud thunder.

（89 技優保甄）

```
al  +  arm
|      |
to + weapon（去拿武器）
```

allow〔ə'laʊ〕v. 允許

We were not *allowed* to wear short skirts
in our school days.（88 南區四技夜二專，89 技優保甄）

anticipate〔æn'tɪsə͵pet〕v. 預期；預料

The museum *anticipates* large crowds on
Sunday, when the new exhibit will open.

（87 四技商專、彰師商教）

```
anti   + cipate
  |        |
beforehand + take（先拿）
```

apologize〔ə'pɑlə͵dʒaɪz〕v. 道歉

When Joe was late for the class, he
apologized to the teacher.（78 師大工教，82 私醫）

自我測驗

- [ ] warrant _____
- [ ] weapon _____
- [ ] wedding _____
- [ ] Wednesday _____
- [ ] young _____

- [ ] accept _____
- [ ] accompany _____
- [ ] achieve _____
- [ ] acquire _____
- [ ] admire _____

- [ ] admit _____
- [ ] affect _____
- [ ] agree _____
- [ ] aim _____
- [ ] allow _____

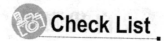

Check List

1.	哨　子	w	_whistle_	e
2.	禮　拜	w		p
3.	優　格	y		t
4.	伴　隨	a		y
5.	累　積	a		e
6.	熟　悉	a		t
7.	獲　得	a		e
8.	使適應	a		t
9.	前　進	a		e
10.	負擔得起	a		d
11.	打　算	a		m
12.	使驚慌	a		m
13.	允　許	a		w
14.	預　期	a		e
15.	道　歉	a		e

appear 〔 ə'pɪr 〕 *v.* 出現

AIDS is caused by a kind of virus, but signs of the disease may not *appear* until several years after a person is infected. (85 保送甄試)

appreciate 〔 ə'priʃɪˌet 〕 *v.* 感激

I really *appreciate* what you have done for me. (88 北區四技夜二專)

```
ap + preci + ate
 |     |     |
to + price + v. ( 對～有好評價 )
```

arrive 〔 ə'raɪv 〕 *v.* 到達

The train starts at five, *arriving* at ten.

(77 台北夜二專)

assume 〔 ə'sum 〕 *v.* 假定；認為

If we receive a call during sleeping hours, we *assume* it is a very important matter.

(79 彰化師大，85 保送甄試)

award 〔ə'wɔrd〕 v. 頒發

Dr. Yang Chen was *awarded* the 1957 Nobel prize for physics. (86中區四技夜二專)

B b

balance 〔'bæləns〕 v. 結算

The teller is *balancing* the customer's account. (89中區夜四技二專)

borrow 〔'baro〕 v. 借入

They're poor but proud. They never *borrow* money or ask for help. (77保送甄試)

bother 〔'baðɚ〕 v. 麻煩;費事

Don't *bother* to lock the door; we'll be back in a minute. (86保送甄試)

breathe 〔brið〕 v. 呼吸

To *breathe* fresh air in the forest is delightful.

(88四技簡專)

C c

calculate〔ˈkælkjəˌlet〕v. 計算

We have to *calculate* the cost of this plan.

（78 保送甄試，88 中區四技夜二專）

calc	+	ul	+ ate
lime	+	small	+ v.

care〔kɛr〕v. 在乎

The old man drinks too much. It seems that he does not *care* about his health.

（82 四技商專、彰化師大，87 台北夜二專）

celebrate〔ˈsɛləˌbret〕v. 慶祝

How do you *celebrate* your birthday?

（88 中區四技夜二專，89 四技二專）

certify〔ˈsɝtəˌfaɪ〕v. 證明

This diploma *certifies* that you have completed high school.

（87 四技商專、彰師商教）

certi	+	fy
sure	+	make

charge 〔 tʃɑrdʒ 〕 v. 收費

The video store *charges* one hundred dollars for each DVD you borrow. (90科大、四技工專)

check 〔 tʃɛk 〕 v. 檢查

Let me *check* your car and see if it is OK.

(85 四技工專、師大工教)

circulate 〔 'sɝkjə,let 〕 v. 使流通

An electric fan is *circulating* the air in the room. (78 四技商專)

collect 〔 kə'lɛkt 〕 v. 收集

She is interested in *collecting* stamps.

(83 保送甄試)

commission 〔 kə'mɪʃən 〕 v. 委託

Margaret was *commissioned* to organize the farewell party. (87 四技商專、彰師商教)

communicate ﹝ kə'mjunə‚ket ﹞ *v.* 溝通

The deaf *communicate* with each other by using body language. (78 保送甄試，82 北區夜二專)

commute ﹝ kə'mjut ﹞ *v.* 通勤

Not all of the students live on campus. Those who live near the university can *commute* by bus. (85 保送甄試)

compel ﹝ kəm'pɛl ﹞ *v.* 強迫

His desire for high grades *compels* him to study every night. (87 四技商專、彰師商教)

compete ﹝ kəm'pit ﹞ *v.* 競爭

Many years ago, woman could hardly *compete* with man outside of the home.

(88 四技商專)

com	+	pete
together	+	*seek*

complain 〔 kəm'plen 〕 *v.* 抱怨

He *complained* that his meal was cold.

（78 師大工教）

computerize 〔 kəm'pjutə‚raɪz 〕 *v.*
使電腦化

Eventually, everything in our life will be
computerized.（78 台北夜二專）

conceal 〔 kən'sil 〕 *v.* 隱藏

I tried to *conceal* my cigarette when the
teacher walked into the room.

（87 四技商專、彰師商教）

confirm 〔 kən'fɝm 〕 *v.* 確認

Please call and *confirm* the ticket you
reserved.（87 南區四技夜二專）

自我測驗

- ☐ appear   _____
- ☐ arrive   _____
- ☐ award   _____
- ☐ borrow   _____
- ☐ bother   _____

- ☐ care   _____
- ☐ celebrate   _____
- ☐ charge   _____
- ☐ check   _____
- ☐ collect   _____

- ☐ commission   _____
- ☐ compel   _____
- ☐ compete   _____
- ☐ computerize   _____
- ☐ confirm   _____

Check List

1.	感　激	a	*appreciate*	e
2.	假　定	a	_____	e
3.	結　算	b	_____	e
4.	麻　煩	b	_____	r
5.	呼　吸	b	_____	e
6.	計　算	c	_____	e
7.	證　明	c	_____	y
8.	收　費	c	_____	e
9.	使流通	c	_____	e
10.	委　託	c	_____	n
11.	溝　通	c	_____	e
12.	通　勤	c	_____	e
13.	競　爭	c	_____	e
14.	抱　怨	c	_____	n
15.	隱　藏	c	_____	l

conserve 〔 kən'sɝv 〕 *v.* 保存;節省

We must *conserve* natural resources so that our children may have a better world to live in. (82 四技工專、師大工教,83 四技商專、彰化師大,84 保送甄試)

con + serve	con + sist
| |	| |
all + *keep*	*all* + *stand*

consist 〔 kən'sɪst 〕 *v.* 組成

It is suggested by doctors that a healthy diet should *consist* of mainly grains, vegetables and fruit with proper amounts of meat and dairy products. (90 科大、四技二專)

consult 〔 kən'sʌlt 〕 *v.* 查閱

When you come across a new word, you may *consult* a dictionary for its meaning.

(78 師大工教)

contact 〔'kɑntækt 〕 *v.* 聯繫

Thank you for applying for the position. The secretary will *contact* you later.（90 科大、四技二專）

contain 〔 kən'ten 〕 *v.* 包含

This book *contains* a lot of fun stuff.

（ 83 保送甄試，89 科大、四技工專，89 中區夜四技二專 ）

contribute 〔 kən'trɪbjut 〕 *v.* 有助於

Proper rest and good sleep *contribute* to longevity.

（ 85 四技商專、彰化師大 ）

con	+ tribute
|	|
together +	*give*

control 〔 kən'trol 〕 *v.* 控制

Stop screaming and try to *control* your temper. （86 台北夜二專）

convey 〔kən've〕 v. 傳達

He sent a card to *convey* his congratulations.

（91 四技二專）

cost 〔kɔst〕 v. 花費

It *costs* a lot to maintain a car in the city.

（80 師大工教）

create 〔krɪ'et〕 v. 創造

He *created* wonderful characters in his novels.（88 中區四技夜二專）

cultivate 〔'kʌltə,vet〕 v. 耕種

This land has been *cultivated* by farmers for generations.（87 保送甄試）

D d

damage 〔'dæmɪdʒ〕 v. 損害

When a road is *damaged*, someone must do the necessary repairs.（82 四技工專、師大工教）

decrease〔dɪ'kris〕*v.* 減少

A research result shows that drinking a lot of water can help *decrease* the risk of developing kidney stones. (83 保送甄試)

delay〔dɪ'le〕*v.* 延誤

I'm sorry I'm late. The plane was *delayed*.

(79 彰化師大，88 南區四技夜二專)

demonstrate〔'dɛmən,stret〕*v.* 示威

The anti-war students took to the streets to *demonstrate* against the war.

(78 保送甄試，82 四技工專、師大工教)

de	+ monstr	+ ate
|	|	|
fully +	*show* +	*v.*

depend 〔 dɪˈpɛnd 〕 v. 取決於

Whether we will have a picnic or not
depends on the weather. (88 科大、四技工專)

deposit 〔 dɪˈpɑzɪt 〕 v. 存（錢）

People *deposit* their money in the bank to
keep it safe. (80 彰化師大)

```
de    + pos + it
 |        |     |
down + put + 物（被置於下方的東西）
```

derive 〔 dəˈraɪv 〕 v. 起源於

Thousands of English words are *derived*
from Latin. (81 台北夜二專)

design 〔 dɪˈzaɪn 〕 v. 設計

Advertising specialists *design* and write
ads for different market segments.

(87 四技商專、彰師商教，89 四技二專)

determine 〔 dɪˈtɝmɪn 〕 *v.* 決心

I am *determined* to go and nothing will

stop me. (79 師大工教，86 中區四技夜二專)

develop 〔 dɪˈvɛləp 〕 *v.* 培養；發展

The aim of true education is to *develop* the

faculties of the mind. (80 台中夜二專)

diagnose 〔 ˌdaɪəgˈnoz 〕 *v.* 診斷

The doctor *diagnosed* his illness as influenza.

(81 台北夜二專)

dial 〔 ˈdaɪəl 〕 *v.* 撥 (電話號碼)

The first step in making a phone call is

dialing the number. (77 四技工專)

differ 〔 ˈdɪfɚ 〕 *v.* 不同；有差異

Although they are twins, they *differ* in

appearance. (90 科大、四技工專)

 自我測驗

- ☐ conserve   _____
- ☐ consist   _____
- ☐ contact   _____
- ☐ contain   _____
- ☐ control   _____

- ☐ cost   _____
- ☐ create   _____
- ☐ damage   _____
- ☐ delay   _____
- ☐ depend   _____

- ☐ derive   _____
- ☐ design   _____
- ☐ develop   _____
- ☐ dial   _____
- ☐ differ   _____

 **Check List**

1. 保　存　　c ___conserve___ e

2. 查　閱　　c _____ t

3. 聯　繫　　c _____ t

4. 包　含　　c _____ n

5. 有助於　　c _____ e

6. 傳　達　　c _____ y

7. 耕　種　　c _____ e

8. 減　少　　d _____ e

9. 示　威　　d _____ e

10. 取決於　　d _____ d

11. 存（錢）　d _____ t

12. 起源於　　d _____ e

13. 決　心　　d _____ e

14. 診　斷　　d _____ e

15. 不　同　　d _____ r

digest〔 daɪˈdʒɛst 〕 *v.* 消化

If you take a walk after dinner, it will help you *digest* the food.（88 北區四技夜二專）

disappear 〔ˌdɪsəˈpɪr 〕 *v.* 消失

The magician made the rabbit *disappear*.

（89 北區四技夜二專）

discover 〔 dɪˈskʌvɚ 〕 *v.* 發現

In the last hundred years, we have *discovered* how to use natural gas for cooking and heating.（88 中區四技夜二專）

dismiss 〔 dɪsˈmɪs 〕 *v.* 解僱

The workers were *dismissed* temporarily from work.（85 台北夜二專）

display 〔 dɪˈsple 〕 *v.* 展示；陳列

If you carry a large sum of cash, don't *display* it openly.（88 中區四技夜二專）

dissolve 〔 dɪˈzɑlv 〕 *v.* 溶解

I watched the sugar *dissolve* as I stirred my tea. (79 四技商專，87 保送甄試)

distinguish 〔 dɪˈstɪŋgwɪʃ 〕 *v.* 辨別

The twins were so much alike that it was impossible to *distinguish* one from the other.

(78 四技商專)

divide 〔 dəˈvaɪd 〕 *v.* 除

Thirty *divided* by three is ten.

(81 四技工專、師大工教、保送甄試，89 中區夜四技二專)

E e

emigrate 〔ˈɛməˌgret 〕 *v.* 移出；移民

Because of the poor economy here, many people have *emigrated*. (86 保送甄試)

e	+ migr	+ ate
|	|	|
out	+ *move*	+ *v.*

encourage 〔 ɪn'kɝɪdʒ 〕 *v.* 鼓勵

Many people worry that the computerized
Public Welfare Lottery *encourages* gambling
instead of working hard to make money.

(83 保送甄試)

enforce 〔 ɪn'fors 〕 *v.* 實施

The government should *enforce* strict laws
to stop people from gambling.

(86 中區四技夜二專)

en	+	force
in	+	力量

enjoy 〔 ɪn'dʒɔɪ 〕 *v.* 喜歡

I have *enjoyed* talking to you about old
times. (79 台北夜二專)

enter 〔 'ɛntɚ 〕 *v.* 進入

Nobody saw the guy *enter* the room.

(77 台北夜二專)

equip 〔 ɪ'kwɪp 〕 v. 裝備；配備

A vehicle *equipped* for transporting sick or injured people is an ambulance. (78 師大工教)

escort 〔'ɛskɔrt 〕 v. 陪同；護送

If the manager is busy with his work, the receptionist should *escort* the visitor to the manager's office. (82 四技商專、彰化師大)

evaporate 〔 ɪ'væpə,ret 〕 v. 蒸發

The water will *evaporate* in the sun.

(89 北區四技夜二專)

exchange 〔 ɪks'tʃendʒ 〕 v. 兌換

You can *exchange* NT dollars at that bank.

(89 四技二專)

exercise 〔'ɛksə,saɪz 〕 v. 運動

They *exercise* every day so they are healthy.

(83 四技工專、師大工教)

exhale 〔 ɛks'hel 〕 *v.* 吐氣

The birthday boy *exhaled* quickly and blew out all the candles. (88 四技二專)

exist 〔 ɪg'zɪst 〕 *v.* 存在

The city library has *existed* since 1947.

(88 中區四技夜二專、南區四技夜二專)

explain 〔 ɪk'splen 〕 *v.* 解釋

I don't understand what you're talking about. Would you *explain* yourself a little?

(77 保送甄試，80 保送甄試)

expose 〔 ɪk'spoz 〕 *v.* 暴露；使接觸

Workers in the factory are *exposed* to poisonous chemicals; therefore, their health is threatened.

(86 保送甄試，88 科大、四技工專)

ex	+	pose
|		|
out	+	*put*

exterminate 〔 ɪk'stɜməˌnet 〕 *v.* 消滅；
根除

This poison will *exterminate* the rats.

（85 四技商專、彰化師大）

extinguish 〔 ɪk'stɪŋgwɪʃ 〕 *v.* 使熄滅

The firemen's job is to *extinguish* fires.

（85 保送甄試）

F f

fasten 〔'fæsn̩〕 *v.* 使牢固

Fasten all the windows and doors before
you go home. （81 台北夜二專）

feed 〔 fid 〕 *v.* 以…為食；餵

Cattle *feed* on grass. （78 保送甄試）

fill 〔 fɪl 〕 *v.* 填寫

You have to *fill* out this application form
before you see the manager. （80 四技商專）

自我測驗

- ☐ disappear _____
- ☐ discover _____
- ☐ dissolve _____
- ☐ encourage _____
- ☐ enforce _____

- ☐ enjoy _____
- ☐ enter _____
- ☐ exchange _____
- ☐ exercise _____
- ☐ exist _____

- ☐ explain _____
- ☐ expose _____
- ☐ fasten _____
- ☐ feed _____
- ☐ fill _____

1. 消　化　　d ___*digest*___ t
2. 消　失　　d _____ r
3. 解　僱　　d _____ s
4. 展　示　　d _____ y
5. 辨　別　　d _____ h

6. 除　　　　d _____ e
7. 移　出　　e _____ e
8. 實　施　　e _____ e
9. 裝　備　　e _____ p
10. 陪　同　　e _____ t

11. 蒸　發　　e _____ e
12. 吐　氣　　e _____ e
13. 消　滅　　e _____ e
14. 使熄滅　　e _____ h
15. 使牢固　　f _____ n

focus 〔'fokəs 〕 v. 集中；集成焦點

Like the eye, the lens can *focus* light from an object onto the film. (80 保送甄試)

G g

gain 〔 gen 〕 v. 增加

If you continue to eat junk food, you will *gain* weight. (90 科大、四技工專)

generate 〔'dʒɛnə‚ret 〕 v. 產生

Lightning is able to *generate* electricity.

(79 彰化師大)

get 〔 gɛt 〕 v. 收到；得到

She *got* a letter from Tom yesterday.

(85 四技工專、師大工教)

grant 〔 grænt 〕 v. 答應

I didn't *grant* him that request.

(87 四技商專、彰師商教)

grate 〔 gret 〕 *v.* 磨碎

Please *grate* some cheese for the pizza.

（87 四技商專、彰師商教）

H h

handle 〔ˈhændḷ〕 *v.* 處理

The situation is too complicated. I can't *handle* it. （81 四技商專）

hesitate 〔ˈhɛzəˌtet〕 *v.* 猶豫

Make up your mind now. Don't *hesitate*!

（89 北區四技夜二專）

hire 〔 haɪr 〕 *v.* 雇用

That company is *hiring* new people. The manager will start to interview people tomorrow. （81 四技商專）

hold (hold) *v.* 舉行

A reception was *held* in honor of the new president. (78 四技商專)

horrify ('hɔrə,faɪ) *v.* 驚嚇

The terrible sight *horrified* everyone.

(78 保送甄試)

I i

identify (aɪ'dɛntə,faɪ) *v.* 辨認

The teacher can easily *identify* the students if they are in uniform. (80 四技商專)

identi	+	fy
the same	+	v.

illustrate ('ɪləstret , ɪ'lʌstret) *v.*
舉例說明

The professor *illustrated* his lecture with diagrams and color slides. (79 彰化師大)

imitate 〔'ɪmə‚tet 〕 v. 模仿

My younger son likes to *imitate* his older brother. (88科大、四技工專)

immigrate 〔'ɪmə‚gret 〕 v. 移入

Do many people *immigrate* to your country?

(86保送甄試)

im	+ migr	+ ate
into	+ move	+ v.

import 〔 ɪm'port 〕 v. 進口

Taiwan *imports* much of its butter and cheese from New Zealand as it doesn't produce enough of them. (86保送甄試)

impress 〔 ɪm'prɛs 〕 v. 使印象深刻

We were greatly *impressed* by his speech.

(81、84四技簡專，84彰師簡教)

im	+ press	
in	+ 壓	(壓進腦海裏)

improve〔ɪm'pruv〕*v.* 改善

To make something better is to *improve* it.

（79 四技工專，83 四技工專、師大工教）

increase〔ɪn'kris〕*v.* 增加

The number of people using dating sites on the Internet *increased* from 3.2 million in June 1999 to 5.6 million in October 2000.

（82 保送甄試，90 科大、四技二專）

infect〔ɪn'fɛkt〕*v.* 感染

Your computer does not work. I'm afraid it has been *infected*. （84 台北夜二專，85 保送甄試）

inflate〔ɪn'flet〕*v.* 充氣

The driver was able to *inflate* the flat tire at the gas station. （91 四技二專）

influence ('ɪnfluəns) *v.* 影響

People say that the crime and violence on TV can *influence* children. (84 保送甄試)

inhabit (ɪn'hæbɪt) *v.* 居住

A family of rabbits *inhabit* the garden behind our house. (88 北區四技夜二專)

inherit (ɪn'hɛrɪt) *v.* 遺傳

She *inherited* her mother's good looks and her father's bad temper. (80 四技工專)

insist (ɪn'sɪst) *v.* 堅持

I *insist* that he stay at home.

(78 保送甄試)

```
in + sist
 |     |
in + stand
```

inspire (ɪn'spaɪr) *v.* 激勵

By the courage and determination expressed in his speeches, he *inspired* the people of Britain to keep on fighting. (82 北區夜二專)

自我測驗

- ☐ focus _____
- ☐ gain _____
- ☐ get _____
- ☐ grant _____
- ☐ handle _____

- ☐ hire _____
- ☐ hold _____
- ☐ identify _____
- ☐ import _____
- ☐ improve _____

- ☐ increase _____
- ☐ infect _____
- ☐ inhabit _____
- ☐ insist _____
- ☐ inspire _____

 **Check List**

1.	集　中	f _____*focus*_____	s
2.	產　生	g _____	e
3.	答　應	g _____	t
4.	磨　碎	g _____	e
5.	猶　豫	h _____	e
6.	驚　嚇	h _____	y
7.	舉例說明	i _____	e
8.	模　仿	i _____	e
9.	移　入	i _____	e
10.	使印象深刻	i _____	s
11.	改　善	i _____	e
12.	增　加	i _____	e
13.	感　染	i _____	t
14.	充　氣	i _____	e
15.	遺　傳	i _____	t

install 〔 ɪn'stɔl 〕 *v.* 裝設

There are over 270,000,000 telephones *installed* throughout the world.

(85 保送甄試，88 科大、四技工專)

insulate 〔'ɪnsə,let 〕 *v.* 隔絕

Her family *insulated* her from contact with the world. (89 科大、四技商專、農科)

insult 〔 ɪn'sʌlt 〕 *v.* 侮辱

You may offer criticism, but be careful not to *insult* the person you are talking to. (88 保送甄試)

intend 〔 ɪn'tɛnd 〕 *v.* 打算；存心

I am sure he didn't *intend* to be insulting to anyone. (78 師大工教)

interfere 〔,ɪntə'fɪr 〕 *v.* 妨礙

If you use your cell phone on an airplane, you may *interfere* with the plane's radio. (88 保送甄試)

invent 〔 ɪn'vɛnt 〕 v. 發明

Alexander Graham Bell *invented* the
telephone in 1876. (77 保送甄試)

involve 〔 ɪn'vɑlv 〕 v. 捲入；涉及

I am sorry to have you *involved* in this matter.

(81 台北夜二專, 83 保送甄試)

irritate 〔 'ɪrə,tet 〕 v. 激怒

The little girl *irritated* her mother by asking
the same question over and over. (88 北區四技夜二專)

isolate 〔 'aɪsḷ,et 〕 v. 使孤立

He *isolated* himself from society. (81 台北夜二專)

K k

kidnap 〔 'kɪdnæp 〕 v. 綁架

The criminal hoped to make a lot of money
by *kidnapping* a rich man. (88 北區四技夜二專)

L l

listen 〔'lɪsn̩〕 *v.* 聽

When children are watching television, they are only *listening* to the language, and they aren't communicating with anyone.

（82 北區夜二專）

lower 〔'loɚ〕 *v.* 放下；降下

An elevator is a suspended cage or car for lifting or *lowering* people or things.

（80 台北夜二專）

M m

maintain 〔men'ten〕 *v.* 保持；維護

Once you buy a car, you have to *maintain* it.

（79 彰化師大，80 師大工教）

manage 〔'mænɪdʒ〕 *v.* 設法

How did you *manage* to get home after you got lost? （80 彰化師大）

manufacture 〔͵mænjə'fæktʃɚ 〕 v. 製造
This factory *manufactures* cars. (91 四技二專)

master 〔'mæstɚ 〕 v. 精通
If you study hard, you can *master* English.

(91 四技二專)

maximize 〔'mæksə͵maɪz 〕 v. 使達到最大 或最高限度
The popular new product will help the company *maximize* its profits. (91 四技二專)

meet 〔 mit 〕 v. 滿足;符合
I took this job because it *meets* my needs.

(89 科大、四技工專)

memorize 〔'mɛmə͵raɪz 〕 v. 背誦;記憶
When you remember a telephone number or an address, you remember because you *memorized* it. (86 南區四技夜二專)

mind 〔 maɪnd 〕 *v.* 介意；在乎

He smokes too much. It seems that he doesn't *mind* his health. (85 台北夜二專)

multiply 〔'mʌltəˌplaɪ 〕 *v.* 繁殖

Some insects grow very fast. They *multiply* rapidly. (81 四技商專)

N n

notice 〔'notɪs 〕 *v.* 注意

Our teacher often told us to *notice* our pronunciation. (85 四技工專、師大工教)

O o

obey 〔 əˈbe 〕 *v.* 遵守

Students are supposed to *obey* school regulations. (85 台北夜二專)

observe 〔 əb'zɝv 〕 v. 觀察

It is interesting to *observe* how students act on the first day at school.

（85 保送甄試，86 台北夜二專，89 科大、四技商專、農專）

```
ob + serve
 |      |
to  + keep（保留在眼前）
```

occur 〔 ə'kɝ 〕 v. 發生

When a plane accident *occurs*, most people are killed. （79 四技商專）

offer 〔'ɔfɚ 〕 v. 提供

Jeff decided to work in this company because it *offered* a better salary.

（85 四技商專、彰化師大，88 科大、四技工專）

operate 〔'ɑpə,ret 〕 v. 操作

He can't make this machine work; he doesn't know how to *operate* it. （87 中區四技夜二專）

 **自我測驗**

- [ ] install　　　＿＿＿＿＿＿＿＿＿＿
- [ ] intend　　　＿＿＿＿＿＿＿＿＿＿
- [ ] invent　　　＿＿＿＿＿＿＿＿＿＿
- [ ] involve　　　＿＿＿＿＿＿＿＿＿＿
- [ ] isolate　　　＿＿＿＿＿＿＿＿＿＿

- [ ] kidnap　　　＿＿＿＿＿＿＿＿＿＿
- [ ] listen　　　＿＿＿＿＿＿＿＿＿＿
- [ ] manage　　　＿＿＿＿＿＿＿＿＿＿
- [ ] master　　　＿＿＿＿＿＿＿＿＿＿
- [ ] maximize　　＿＿＿＿＿＿＿＿＿＿

- [ ] mind　　　　＿＿＿＿＿＿＿＿＿＿
- [ ] notice　　　＿＿＿＿＿＿＿＿＿＿
- [ ] obey　　　　＿＿＿＿＿＿＿＿＿＿
- [ ] occur　　　＿＿＿＿＿＿＿＿＿＿
- [ ] offer　　　＿＿＿＿＿＿＿＿＿＿

Check List

1.	裝　設	i _____*install*_____	l
2.	隔　絕	i _____	e
3.	侮　辱	i _____	t
4.	妨　礙	i _____	e
5.	激　怒	i _____	e
6.	使孤立	i _____	e
7.	放　下	l _____	r
8.	保　持	m _____	n
9.	製　造	m _____	e
10.	滿　足	m _____	t
11.	背　誦	m _____	e
12.	繁　殖	m _____	y
13.	觀　察	o _____	e
14.	發　生	o _____	r
15.	操　作	o _____	e

organize ﹝'ɔrgən‚aɪz﹞ *v.* 組織

Our school is trying to *organize* a baseball team. (78 四技工專，85 保送甄試)

overcome ﹝‚ovɚ'kʌm﹞ *v.* 克服

A friendly smile helps us make friends quickly and *overcomes* differences in customs. (80 台中夜二專)

P p

paint ﹝ pent ﹞ *v.* 油漆

He is about to *paint* his bedroom. (79 保送甄試)

participate ﹝ pɚ'tɪsə‚pet ﹞ *v.* 參與

In a modern democracy people want to *participate* more fully. (87 四技商專、彰師商教)

perform ﹝ pɚ'fɔrm ﹞ *v.* 執行；做

Electronic calculators can *perform* very complex operations. (77 四技工專)

personify 〔 pɚˈsɑnəˌfaɪ 〕 *v.* 擬人化

We often *personify* the sun and the moon.

（78 台北夜二專）

persuade 〔 pɚˈswed 〕 *v.* 說服

He was such a stubborn man that I could not *persuade* him to give up that plan. （80 彰化師大）

per	+ suade
|	|
thoroughly	+ *advise*

postpone 〔 postˈpon 〕 *v.* 延期

Today's football match has been *postponed* because of bad weather. They will play next Friday instead. （84 四技簡專、彰師簡教）

pour 〔 por 〕 *v.* 傾倒

Can I *pour* some more coffee for you?

（88 四技二專）

practice (ˈpræktɪs) *v.* 以…爲業

The physician started to *practice* medicine
as early as 1960. (78師大工教)

predict (prɪˈdɪkt) *v.* 預測

It is *predicted* that there will be a great
earthquake in the near
future. (84台北夜二專)

pre	+ dict
before	+ say

prefer (prɪˈfɝ) *v.* 比較喜歡

He *prefers* a new house to a remodeled one.

(84保送甄試)

preserve (prɪˈzɝv) *v.* 保存

Drying is one of the oldest known ways
of *preserving* fruits.

(86保送甄試)

pre	+ serve
before	+ keep

prevent 〔 prɪ'vɛnt 〕 v. 阻止

If you *prevent* someone from doing something, you stop him from doing it.

（79 保送甄試，83 四技工專、師大工敎，89 中區夜四技二專）

```
pre  + vent
  |      |
before + come （先到達做準備）
```

promote 〔 prə'mot 〕 v. 促銷

Many companies use television advertisements to *promote* their products.

（91 四技二專）

```
pro   + mote
  |       |
forward + move （向前移動）
```

protect 〔 prə'tɛkt 〕 v. 保護

Parents try their best to *protect* their children from getting hurt.

（78 四技商專，82 保送甄試）

```
pro + tect
  |      |
before + cover
```

provide〔 prə'vaɪd 〕 *v.* 提供

In primitive societies people used to *provide* all the things they needed themselves.

（ 83 保送甄試 ）

R r

raise〔 rez 〕 *v.* 提高

The postal service won't get away easily with *raising* postal rates this time. （ 80 師大工教 ）

recognize〔'rɛkə,naɪz 〕 *v.* 認出

My English teacher had changed so much that I almost did not *recognize* her.

（ 80 彰化師大，85 保送甄試，88 北區四技夜二專 ）

recycle〔 ri'saɪkḷ 〕 *v.* 回收

Pollution can be greatly reduced when solid wastes such as glass bottles, old automobile tires and newspapers are *recycled*.

（ 84 保送甄試，89 北區四技夜二專 ）

reduce 〔rɪˈdjus〕 *v.* 減少

Garbage has become a serious problem.
We should *reduce* the number of plastic
bags used. (86 台北夜二專)

```
re   + duce
 |      |
back + lead (引導回歸)
```

refine 〔rɪˈfaɪn〕 *v.* 使…優雅

Yoy must *refine* your manners. (89 北區四技夜二專)

refuse 〔rɪˈfjuz〕 *v.* 拒絕

If you *refuse* to help others, they may not
help you. (89 技優保甄)

relax 〔rɪˈlæks〕 *v.* 放鬆

After we shopped all day, it was nice to sit
down in a coffee shop and *relax*. (86 南區四技夜二專)

自我測驗

- ☐ overcome   _____
- ☐ paint   _____
- ☐ perform   _____
- ☐ personify   _____
- ☐ pour   _____

- ☐ practice   _____
- ☐ predict   _____
- ☐ prefer   _____
- ☐ prevent   _____
- ☐ promote   _____

- ☐ provide   _____
- ☐ raise   _____
- ☐ recognize   _____
- ☐ reduce   _____
- ☐ refuse   _____

 **Check List**

1. 組　織　o ___organize___ e
2. 克　服　o _____ e
3. 參　與　p _____ e
4. 執　行　p _____ m
5. 擬人化　p _____ y

6. 說　服　p _____ e
7. 延　期　p _____ e
8. 預　測　p _____ t
9. 保　存　p _____ e
10. 保　護　p _____ t

11. 認　出　r _____ e
12. 回　收　r _____ e
13. 減　少　r _____ e
14. 使優雅　r _____ e
15. 放　鬆　r _____ x

release 〔 rɪ'lis 〕 v. 釋放

The sun *releases* large amounts of solar energy to the earth every minute. (89 技優保甄)

remember 〔 rɪ'mɛmbɚ 〕 v. 記得

It was very considerate of you to *remember* her birthday. (81 四技商專)

remove 〔 rɪ'muv 〕 v. 除去

Scientists are trying to turn seawater drinking water by *removing* the salt.

(87 保送甄試)

replace 〔 rɪ'ples 〕 v. 取代

Nothing can *replace* a mother's love and care.

(82 嘉南、高屏區夜二專，82 四技商專、彰化師大)

reply 〔 rɪ'plaɪ 〕 v. 回答；回信

I sent Mary a letter last week, but she has not *replied*. (89 北區四技夜二專)

report 〔 rɪ'port 〕 v. 報導

It is *reported* that the general election will be held soon. (78 四技商專)

represent 〔 ˌrɛprɪ'zɛnt 〕 v. 代表

CPR *represents* cardiopulmonary resuscitation. (83 北區夜二專)

repute 〔 rɪ'pjut 〕 v. 認為

He was *reputed* to be a very learned scholar but actually he was a fake. (79 台北夜二專)

require 〔 rɪ'kwaɪr 〕 v. 需要

An employer usually *requires* an interview before hiring a job seeker. (80 台中夜二專)

re	+ quire
again	+ *seek*

resign 〔 rɪ'zaɪn 〕 v. 辭職

After the serious argument, he *resigned* from
the post and left the company.

（81 台北夜二專，86 中區四技夜二專）

respond 〔 rɪ'spɑnd 〕 v. 反應

Your printer is not *responding*. You haven't
hooked it up to the computer. （83 保送甄試）

$$
\begin{array}{c}
re \ + spond \\
| \quad\quad | \\
back \ + promise
\end{array}
$$

result 〔 rɪ'zʌlt 〕 v. 產生

Sickness often *results* from eating too much.

（83 保送甄試）

return 〔 rɪ't3n 〕 v. 歸還

Please *return* these books to the library.

（90 科大、四技工專）

revolutionize 〔,rɛvə'luʃən,aɪz 〕 *v.*
徹底改革

Sports advertising has *revolutionized* the
field of marketing in the USA. (87中區四技夜二專)

revolve 〔 rɪ'vɑlv 〕 *v.* 旋轉;公轉

It's a fact that the earth *revolves* around the
sun. (89科大、四技商、農專)

reward 〔 rɪ'wɔrd 〕 *v.* 酬謝

The honest boy was *rewarded* for returning
the wallet to its owner. (91四技二專)

rotate 〔'rotet 〕 *v.* 輪耕

Farmers often *rotate* forage crops with other
crops to help enrich the soil and to prevent
soil erosion. (87保送甄試)

S s

satisfy ('sætɪs,faɪ) *v.* 滿足

Gina gets good grades in mathematics, but that can not *satisfy* her parents.

（83 四技工專、師大工教）

serve (sɝv) *v.* 滿足

Modern department stores *serve* the needs of entire families. （78 四技商專，86 南區四技夜二專）

set (sɛt) *v.* 創（紀錄）

Many people around the world want to *set* new records in all kinds of activities so that their names can be entered into the Guinness Book. （85 保送甄試）

shake (ʃek) *v.* 握（手）；搖動

It is polite to *shake* someone's hand when you meet him. （89 科大、四技商專、農科）

shrink (ʃrɪŋk) *v.* 縮小

The vast forests of Brazil have been *shrinking* due to exploitation. (88 保送甄試)

sniff (snɪf) *v.* 嗅

The dog *sniffed* around and then started running again. (79 彰化師大)

solve (salv) *v.* 解決

Besides gathering and storing information, the computer can also *solve* complicated problems. (79 彰化師大)

specialize (ˈspɛʃəlˌaɪz) *v.* 專攻

After completing medical school, the doctor decided to *specialize* in heart surgery.

(91 四技二專)

 **自我測驗**

- [ ] remember _____
- [ ] replace _____
- [ ] reply _____
- [ ] report _____
- [ ] require _____

- [ ] resign _____
- [ ] respond _____
- [ ] result _____
- [ ] return _____
- [ ] reward _____

- [ ] serve _____
- [ ] set _____
- [ ] shake _____
- [ ] shrink _____
- [ ] solve _____

Check List

1. 釋　放　　r ____*release*____ e

2. 除　去　　r _____ e

3. 取　代　　r _____ e

4. 代　表　　r _____ t

5. 認　為　　r _____ e

6. 反　應　　r _____ d

7. 徹底改革　r _____ e

8. 旋　轉　　r _____ e

9. 酬　謝　　r _____ d

10. 輪　耕　　r _____ e

11. 滿　足　　s _____ y

12. 縮　小　　s _____ k

13. 嗅　　　　s _____ f

14. 解　決　　s _____ e

15. 專　攻　　s _____ e

spell 〔 spɛl 〕 *v.* 拼（字）

The teacher asked him to *spell* the word
"potato."（81 四技工專、師大工教）

spend 〔 spɛnd 〕 *v.* 花費

If you shop in this expensive store, you will
spend a lot of money.（88 科大、四技工專）

spill 〔 spɪl 〕 *v.* 灑出

Be careful. I *spilt* some water and the floor
is slippery.（88 四技二專）

split 〔 splɪt 〕 *v.* 平均分攤

Let's *split* the bill rather than fight over who
should pay.（88 四技二專）

spoil 〔 spɔɪl 〕 *v.* 腐敗

Fish *spoils* quickly in the sun.（80 四技工專）

squeeze 〔 skwiz 〕 *v.* 擠壓

Please don't *squeeze* the mangoes unless you are going to buy them. (87 保送甄試)

stand 〔 stænd 〕 *v.* 忍受

I just can't *stand* the hot weather here.

(82 嘉南、高屏區夜二專)

starve 〔 stɑrv 〕 *v.* 飢餓

Without food we would *starve* to death.

(85 保送甄試)

steer 〔 stɪr 〕 *v.* 駕駛

Keep both hands on the wheel when you are *steering* the car. (87 四技商專、彰師商教)

strain 〔 stren 〕 *v.* (因過度使用而) 損傷

Don't *strain* your eyes by reading or working in a dim light. (77 四技商專)

strengthen 〔'strɛŋθən 〕 v. 加強

A person who thinks he is incapable tends
to fail. Moreover, failure
will *strengthen* his belief
in his incompetence.

（78 四技商專，83 北區夜二專）

stride 〔 straɪd 〕 v. 大步行走

We knew he was angry by the way he had
stridden into the room. （88 四技二專）

submit 〔 səb'mɪt 〕 v. 繳交；屈服

The teacher said we may *submit* our papers
by email. （87 保送甄試）

```
  sub  + mit
   |      |
under + send （從下面過去）
```

subtract 〔 səb'trækt 〕 v. 減去

If you *subtract* 8 from 15, you will have 7.

（78 四技商專）

succeed 〔sək'sid〕 v. 成功

If you work hard, you will *succeed*. （78 台北夜二專）

```
┌──────────────────┐  ┌──────────────────┐
│  suc  + ceed     │  │  suf  + fer      │
│   │     │        │  │   │     │        │
│ under + go       │  │ under + bear     │
└──────────────────┘  └──────────────────┘
```

suffer 〔'sʌfɚ〕 v. 遭受；罹患

Mary has a cold. She *suffers* from a
headache. （79 保送甄試）

summarize 〔'sʌmə,raɪz〕 v. 扼要說明

Headlines usually briefly *summarize* the
news stories, so they can help the reader
decide quickly what to read, skim, or ignore.

（82 四技商專、彰化師大）

suppose 〔sə'poz〕 v. 假定；若是

Suppose he refuses, what shall we do?

（79、85 台北夜二專，86 中區四技夜二專，88 四技商專）

surrender 〔 səˈrɛndə 〕 v. 投降

The general said he would never *surrender* to the enemy. (89科大、四技簡專、農科)

survey 〔 səˈve 〕 v. 調查

The police *survyed* the scene of the crime carefully for fear of missing any clue that was related to the murder. (90科大、四技二專)

survive 〔 səˈvaɪv 〕 v. 自…中生還

Only one little girl *survived* the accident; everyone else was killed. (80四技工專)

T t

transcend 〔 trænˈsɛnd 〕 v. 超越

Your parents' love for you *transcends* reason; they will love you no matter what.

(89科大、四技簡專、農科)

transcribe 〔 træn'skraɪb 〕 *v.* 抄寫

The reporter recorded the interview and then *transcribed* it into his notebook.

（89科大、四技商專、農科）

transmit 〔 træns'mɪt 〕 *v.* 傳染

This kind of virus is *transmitted* by personal contact.

（89科大、四技商專、農專）

```
trans  + mit
  |        |
across + send
```

transport 〔 træns'port 〕 *v.* 運輸

The cars are *transported* by ship. （89技優保甄）

U u

undergo 〔 ˌʌndɚ'go 〕 *v.* 經歷

The explorers had to *undergo* much suffering and even some dangers. （80四技工專）

自我測驗

- [ ] spell _____
- [ ] spend _____
- [ ] split _____
- [ ] spoil _____
- [ ] stand _____

- [ ] starve _____
- [ ] strain _____
- [ ] stride _____
- [ ] submit _____
- [ ] succeed _____

- [ ] suffer _____
- [ ] survey _____
- [ ] survive _____
- [ ] transcend _____
- [ ] transcribe _____

 **Check List**

1. 灑 出	s	_spill_	l
2. 擠 壓	s		e
3. 忍 受	s		d
4. 駕 駛	s		r
5. 加 強	s		n
6. 大步行走	s		e
7. 減 去	s		t
8. 扼要說明	s		e
9. 假 定	s		e
10. 投 降	s		r
11. 自…中生還	s		e
12. 超 越	t		d
13. 抄 寫	t		e
14. 傳 染	t		t
15. 經 歷	u		o

understand 〔͵ʌndɚˈstænd〕 v. 了解

She could not make herself *understood*.

（77 台北夜二專）

V v

visit 〔ˈvɪzɪt〕 v. 拜訪

It is suggested by the workers in the zoo that it is best to *visit* the bears at an early hour, when they are most active. （90 科大、四技二專）

vomit 〔ˈvɑmɪt〕 v. 嘔吐

The little girl was seasick and started to *vomit* everything she had eaten. （87 保送甄試）

W w

wag 〔wæg〕 v. 搖擺

Our dog *wags* its tail when it sees us coming from school. （89 技優保甄）

wake 〔 wek 〕 v. 叫醒

Be quiet or you will *wake* the baby. (89 技優保甄)

warn 〔 wɔrn 〕 v. 警告

The smoke alarm will *warn* you when there is a fire in the building. (89 四技二專)

waste 〔 west 〕 v. 浪費

Traffic jams *waste* a lot of time. (89 技優保甄)

wear 〔 wɛr 〕 v. 穿；戴

Our principal is a little man who *wears* thick glasses. (85 四技工專、師大工教)

withdraw 〔 wɪð'drɔ 〕 v. 提 (款)

Customers can *withdraw* money from 24-hour banking machines.

(88 北區四技夜二專)

```
with  +  draw
  |        |
back  +   拉
```

wither ('wɪðɚ) *v.* 枯萎

Corn *withered* and dropped because of the drought. (84 保送甄試)

worry ('wɝɪ) *v.* 擔心

Don't *worry* about me. Everything will be fine. (87 台北夜二專)

形容詞

abrupt 〔 ə'brʌpt 〕 *adj.* 突然的

The taxi came to an *abrupt* stop when the traffic light turned red. (88 四技二專)

accurate 〔'ækjərɪt 〕 *adj.* 準確的

Your typing is not very fast but it is *accurate*.

(77 四技商專)

```
ac + cur + ate
|     |     |
to + care + adj.
```

adequate 〔'ædəkwɪt 〕 *adj.* 足夠的

The food we have prepared is not *adequate* for the number of people at the party.

(87 四技商專、彰師商教，88 北區四技夜二專)

admirable 〔'ædmərəbḷ 〕 *adj.* 值得稱讚的

Honesty is an *admirable* characteristic.

(78 師大工教)

affordable 〔 əˋfɔrdəbḷ 〕 *adj.* 負擔得起的

Many researchers are trying to improve the design of electric cars and make them more *affordable*. (88 中區四技夜二專)

agreeable 〔 əˋgriəbḷ 〕 *adj.* 令人愉快的

How can you create an *agreeable* conversation? (78 四技商專)

agricultural 〔 ͵ægrɪˋkʌltʃərəl 〕 *adj.* 農業的

We should learn how to improve our *agricultural* output by using better methods and tools. (82 保送甄試)

alike 〔 əˋlaɪk 〕 *adj.* 相似的

The two sisters look very much *alike*.

(88 中區四技夜二專)

alive 〔 ə'laɪv 〕 *adj.* 活的

People have a better chance of remaining *alive* in a car accident if they use seat belts.

（79 四技商專）

allergic 〔 ə'lɝdʒɪk 〕 *adj.* 過敏的

Judy is *allergic* to seafood. When she has seafood, she feels uncomfortable.

（86 保送甄試，88 四技商專）

ambitious 〔 æm'bɪʃəs 〕 *adj.* 有野心的

Bob is very *ambitious*; he hopes to run his own company one day. （87 四技商專、彰師商教）

amusing 〔 ə'mjuzɪŋ 〕 *adj.* 有趣的

The TV program is *amusing*. （85 台北夜二專）

ancient 〔'enʃənt 〕 *adj.* 古代的

Museums have *ancient* and modern art.

（87 四技商專、彰師商教）

 自我測驗

- [ ] understand　　＿＿＿＿＿＿＿＿＿
- [ ] visit　　＿＿＿＿＿＿＿＿＿
- [ ] wag　　＿＿＿＿＿＿＿＿＿
- [ ] wake　　＿＿＿＿＿＿＿＿＿
- [ ] waste　　＿＿＿＿＿＿＿＿＿

- [ ] wear　　＿＿＿＿＿＿＿＿＿
- [ ] wither　　＿＿＿＿＿＿＿＿＿
- [ ] worry　　＿＿＿＿＿＿＿＿＿
- [ ] abrupt　　＿＿＿＿＿＿＿＿＿
- [ ] adequate　　＿＿＿＿＿＿＿＿＿

- [ ] agreeable　　＿＿＿＿＿＿＿＿＿
- [ ] alike　　＿＿＿＿＿＿＿＿＿
- [ ] alive　　＿＿＿＿＿＿＿＿＿
- [ ] amusing　　＿＿＿＿＿＿＿＿＿
- [ ] ancient　　＿＿＿＿＿＿＿＿＿

 **Check List**

1. 嘔　吐　　　v _____vomit_____ t
2. 搖　擺　　　w _____ g
3. 警　告　　　w _____ n
4. 提（款）　　w _____ w
5. 枯　萎　　　w _____ r

6. 準確的　　　a _____ e
7. 足夠的　　　a _____ e
8. 值得稱讚的　a _____ e
9. 負擔得起的　a _____ e
10. 令人愉快的　a _____ e

11. 農業的　　　a _____ l
12. 活　的　　　a _____ e
13. 過敏的　　　a _____ c
14. 有野心的　　a _____ s
15. 古代的　　　a _____ t

annual ('ænjʊəl) *adj.* 一年的；一年一次的

That contract is effective for only one year;
it is an *annual* one. (88 四技商專)

artificial (ˌɑrtə'fɪʃəl) *adj.* 人造的

The *artificial* flowers look almost real.

(88 保送甄試)

art	+ fic	+ ial
skill	+ make	+ adj.

asleep (ə'slip) *adj.* 睡著的

As soon as Mary went to bed, she was able
to fall *asleep*.

(86 南區四技夜二專)

a	+ sleep
in	+ 睡覺

automatic (ˌɔtə'mætɪk) *adj.* 自動的

You can withdraw the money from the
automatic teller machine at any time.

(88 中區四技夜二專)

available 〔 ə'veləbḷ 〕 *adj.* 可獲得的

The hotel is full. There are no rooms *available*.

（81 四技商專，82 嘉南、高屏區夜二專，86 保送甄試，89 四技二專）

average 〔'ævərɪdʒ 〕 *adj.* 平均的

Although only of *average* intelligence, he speaks three languages fluently.

（84 四技商專、彰師商教）

aware 〔 ə'wɛr 〕 *adj.* 知道的；察覺到的

A good salesperson is *aware* of his strengths and weaknesses, and constantly tries to improve his sales skills. （84 保送甄試）

B b

basic 〔'besɪk 〕 *adj.* 基本的

Buses are the *basic* transportation for students in the city. （88 四技商專）

beautiful 〔'bjutəfəl 〕 *adj.* 漂亮的

Miss Brown is really a *beautiful* lady.

（80 師大工教，85 四技工專、師大工教）

believable 〔 bɪ'livəbḷ 〕 *adj.* 可信的

The story she told us is really highly
believable. （87 中區四技夜二專）

brief 〔 brif 〕 *adj.* 簡短的

When writing a memorandum, be sure that it
is *brief* and to the point. （86 台北夜二專）

broken 〔'brokən 〕 *adj.* 破碎的

John and his wife are no longer living
together. They have a *broken* marriage.

（77 保送甄試）

C c

careful 〔'kɛrfəl 〕 *adj.* 小心的

One has to be very *careful* when he is asked
to make a very formal speech. （80 四技工專）

carnivorous (kɑr'nɪvərəs) *adj.* 肉食的

Tigers and lions are *carnivorous* animals.

(78 保送甄試)

challenging ('tʃælɪndʒɪŋ) *adj.* 具挑戰性的

Scientists today are faced with the most *challenging* task of developing a vaccine against AIDS. (84 保送甄試)

chronic ('krɑnɪk) *adj.* 慢性的

The old man must never work too hard because he has a *chronic* heart disease.

(86 保送甄試)

```
chron + ic
  |      |
 time  + adj. (耗費時間的)
```

cleanly ('klɛnlɪ) *adj.* 愛乾淨的

The cat is a *cleanly* animal. (77 台北夜二專)

common ('kɑmən) *adj.* 普通的；常見的

This case is *common*, nothing special.

（82 保送甄試，85 台北夜二專）

communicable (kə'mjunɪkəbḷ) *adj.*
可傳染的

If the patient has a *communicable* disease,
the doctor may order that he be isolated.

（82 四技商專、彰化師大）

compact (kəm'pækt) *adj.* 小型的；
輕便的

Henry has a very good *compact* disc player.

（89 中區夜四技二專）

competitive (kəm'pɛtətɪv) *adj.*
競爭激烈的

We will have a *competitive* examination
next Monday. （79 四技商專，80 台北夜二專）

complimentary 〔͵kɑmpləˋmɛntərɪ〕*adj.*
問候的

The most common *complimentary* close that
we use in English letters is "Sincerely."

（85 四技商專、彰化師大）

compulsive 〔kəmˋpʌlsɪv〕*adj.* 衝動的

Paul is a *compulsive* bargain hunter. He
often buys things not because he needs
them but only because they are cheap.

（84 四技商專、彰師商教）

concentrated 〔ˋkɑnsn͵tretɪd〕*adj.* 濃縮
的；集中的

The drink is made from wine mixed with
concentrated orange juice.（86 中區四技夜二專）

concise 〔kənˋsaɪs〕*adj.* 簡明的

A good letter should be clear, *concise* and
courteous.（78 四技商專）

 自我測驗

- ☐ annual _____
- ☐ asleep _____
- ☐ average _____
- ☐ aware _____
- ☐ beautiful _____

- ☐ broken _____
- ☐ careful _____
- ☐ challenging _____
- ☐ chronic _____
- ☐ cleanly _____

- ☐ common _____
- ☐ compact _____
- ☐ compulsive _____
- ☐ concentrated _____
- ☐ concise _____

Check List

1. 人造的　　　a ___artificial___ l
2. 自動的　　　a _____ c
3. 可獲得的　　a _____ e
4. 可信的　　　b _____ e
5. 簡短的　　　b _____ f
6. 破碎的　　　b _____ n
7. 肉食的　　　c _____ s
8. 慢性的　　　c _____ c
9. 可傳染的　　c _____ e
10. 小型的　　　c _____ t
11. 競爭激烈的　c _____ e
12. 問候的　　　c _____ y
13. 衝動的　　　c _____ e
14. 濃縮的　　　c _____ d
15. 簡明的　　　c _____ e

confused 〔 kən'fjuzd 〕 *adj.* 困惑的

The students were *confused* by the teacher's answer, but acted as if they understood.

（88 科大、四技工專）

consequent 〔'kɑnsə,kwɛnt 〕 *adj.* 接著發生的

In the *consequent* confusion after the earthquake, many fires broke out.

（77 台北夜二專）

conservative 〔 kən'sɝvətɪv 〕 *adj.* 保守的

Chinese parents are so *conservative* that they feel embarrassed to teach their children about sex. （83 保送甄試）

considerate 〔 kən'sɪdərɪt 〕 *adj.* 體貼的

It is very *considerate* of you to come to see me.

（80 台北夜二專、師大工教，81 四技商專）

```
consider + ate
   |         |
  考慮   + adj.
```

content 〔 kən'tɛnt 〕 *adj.* 滿足的

Mary is happy with her life. She's *content*.

（82 嘉南、高屏區夜二專）

continual 〔 kən'tɪnjuəl 〕 *adj.* 持續的

I can't stand the *continual* noise in the classroom. （89 中區夜四技二專）

convinced 〔 kən'vɪnst 〕 *adj.* 確信的

All of us are *convinced* that she is guilty.

（86 中區四技夜二專）

creative 〔 krɪ'etɪv 〕 *adj.* 有創造力的

Tom is a very *creative* boy; he always has neat ideas. （80 四技商專）

crowded 〔'kraʊdɪd 〕 *adj.* 擁擠的

The department store is very *crowded*. There are many people inside. （77 師大工教）

crucial 〔ˈkruʃəl 〕 *adj.* 非常重要的

It is *crucial* to prepare well before a typhoon.

（88 四技二專）

cultural 〔ˈkʌltʃərəl 〕 *adj.* 文化的

In ancient Greece, Athens was considered to be the *cultural* capital of the world. （79 師大工教）

D d

dangerous 〔ˈdendʒərəs 〕 *adj.* 危險的

Though the lion is *dangerous*, hunters still hunt for it in the wilderness.

（82 私醫）

danger	+ ous
危險	+ *adj.*

dead 〔 dɛd 〕 *adj.* 死的

His father has been *dead* for nearly ten years. （87 中區四技夜二專）

debatable 〔 dɪ'betəbḷ 〕 *adj.* 有爭議的

Nowadays, nuclear energy is a *debatable* issue. (85 台北夜二專)

defective 〔 dɪ'fɛktɪv 〕 *adj.* 有缺陷的

This pen is *defective*; it won't write.

(89 科大、四技商專、農科)

delicious 〔 dɪ'lɪʃəs 〕 *adj.* 美味的

Some people consider beef noodles cheaper and more *delicious* than American food such as hamburgers. (77 師大工教)

delighted 〔 dɪ'laɪtɪd 〕 *adj.* 高興的

Mother was *delighted* with the present we gave her. (88 保送甄試)

dependable 〔 dɪ'pɛndəbḷ 〕 *adj.* 可靠的

My car is always breaking down; I should buy a more *dependable* one. (86 保送甄試)

dependent 〔 dɪ'pɛndənt 〕 *adj.* 視～而定的；依賴的

Our trip is *dependent* on the weather.

（83 保送甄試）

depressed 〔 dɪ'prɛst 〕 *adj.* 沮喪的

I feel very *depressed* by the bad news.

（79 彰化師大）

destructive 〔 dɪ'strʌktɪv 〕 *adj.* 破壞性的

The *destructive* typhoon damaged many people's homes. （89 科大、四技商專、農科）

detailed 〔 'diteld 〕 *adj.* 詳細的

The police made a *detailed* investigation of the murder. （88 保送甄試）

different 〔 'dɪfərənt 〕 *adj.* 不同的

I often go to the international club to meet people from *different*
countries. （88 保送甄試）

```
differ + ent
  |       |
不同   + adj.
```

disabled 〔 dɪsˈebl̩d 〕 *adj.* 殘障的

This is a special school for the physically *disabled*. (85 台北夜二專)

disgusted 〔 dɪsˈgʌstɪd 〕 *adj.* 覺得噁心的

We were *disgusted* by the terrible food in the cafeteria. (86 保送甄試)

disgusting 〔 dɪsˈgʌstɪŋ 〕 *adj.* 令人厭惡的

People will feel offended when someone makes *disgusting* remarks to them. (80 四技工專)

dissatisfied 〔 dɪsˈsætɪsˌfaɪd 〕 *adj.* 不滿意的

Some have always been *dissatisfied* with things as they are. (80 師大工教)

domestic 〔 dəˈmɛstɪk 〕 *adj.* 國內的

We are going to take a *domestic* flight to Tainan. (81 四技商專)

# 自我測驗

☐ confuse _____

☐ conservative _____

☐ content _____

☐ creative _____

☐ cultural _____

☐ dangerous _____

☐ dead _____

☐ delicious _____

☐ delighted _____

☐ dependent _____

☐ detailed _____

☐ different _____

☐ disgusted _____

☐ dissatisfied _____

☐ domestic _____

 **Check List**

1. 接著發生的　　c _consequent_ t

2. 體貼的　　　　c _____ e

3. 持續的　　　　c _____ l

4. 確信的　　　　c _____ d

5. 非常重要的　　c _____ l

6. 有爭議的　　　d _____ e

7. 有缺陷的　　　d _____ e

8. 美味的　　　　d _____ s

9. 可依靠的　　　d _____ e

10. 沮喪的　　　　d _____ d

11. 破壞性的　　　d _____ e

12. 詳細的　　　　d _____ d

13. 殘障的　　　　d _____ d

14. 令人厭惡的　　d _____ g

15. 國內的　　　　d _____ c

doubtful ﹝ˈdaʊtfəl﹞ *adj.* 懷疑的

It is such a sunny day that I am *doubtful* it will rain later. (88 保送甄試)

dull ﹝dʌl﹞ *adj.* 鈍的

This knife is so *dull* that it won't even cut a slice of bread. (88 保送甄試)

durable ﹝ˈdjʊrəbḷ﹞ *adj.* 耐久的

When times are good and incomes high, *durable* goods will have the greatest increase in sales. (88 保送甄試)

```
dur     + able
 |          |
lasting  +  adj.
```

E e

eager ﹝ˈigɚ﹞ *adj.* 渴望的；急切的

The birthday boy was so *eager* to open his present that he even forgot to say thank you.

(89 科大、四技工專)

economic (ˌikə'nɑmɪk) *adj.* 經濟的

An *economic* system must settle the questions of what goods shall be produced and who shall get them. (88 保送甄試)

educational (ˌɛdʒə'keʃənl̩) *adj.* 教育的

Television has a good influence on children when it can offer *educational* programs for them. (85 四技商專、彰化師大)

effective (ə'fɛktɪv) *adj.* 有效的

The government should take some *effective* measures to solve the problem.

(89 科大、四技商專、農專)

```
ef  + fect + ive
 |     |      |
out + make + adj.
```

elder ('ɛldə) *adj.* 年紀較大的

The girl and her *elder* sister look so much alike that the neighbors can hardly tell them apart. (90 科大、四技二專)

essential ﹝ əˈsɛnʃəl ﹞ *adj.* 必要的

Food and water are *essential* to life.

（77 四技商專，82 四技工專、師大工教，84 台北夜二專）

evil ﹝ ˈivl̩ ﹞ *adj.* 邪惡的

The people were finally able to overthrow the *evil* ruler. （89 四技二專）

exact ﹝ ɪgˈzækt ﹞ *adj.* 準確的；恰好的

Being on time and organizing everything by *exact* time is important in modern society.

（85 保送甄試）

excellent ﹝ ˈɛksl̩ənt ﹞ *adj.* 優秀的；極好的

Mary was delighted when she received an *excellent* grade on the history paper.

（90 科大、四技工專）

excited ﹝ ɪkˈsaɪtɪd ﹞ *adj.* 感到興奮的

I am not very *excited* about the news.

（82 保送甄試）

exclusive 〔 ɪkˈsklusɪv 〕 *adj.* 獨有的

The inventor has the *exclusive* right to make what he has invented and patented for a certain number of years. (79 彰化師大)

exhausted 〔 ɪgˈzɔstɪd 〕 *adj.* 筋疲力盡的

They felt quite *exhausted*.

(79 保送甄試，83 四技商專、彰化師大)

extinct 〔 ɪkˈstɪŋkt 〕 *adj.* 絕種的

If we don't take care of the countryside, many more animals will become *extinct*.

(84 四技商專、彰師簡教)

F f

familiar 〔 fəˈmɪljə 〕 *adj.* 熟悉的

I am not *familiar* with this song. Do you know who the singer is?

(88 科大、四技工專)

famili + ar
| |
family + *adj.*

famous ('feməs) *adj.* 有名的

Hawaii is particularly *famous* for its
beautiful weather. (80 師大工教)

far (fɑr) *adj.* 遠的

How *far* is it from here to the shopping
center? (79 師大工教)

favorite ('fevərɪt) *adj.* 最喜愛的

"Hershey's" is my *favorite* type of chocolate.
I love it above all others. (77 保送甄試)

fertile ('fɜtḷ) *adj.* 肥沃的

The land here is so *fertile* that the farmers
can grow three crops a year.

(87 保送甄試)

```
fert  +  ile
 |        |
bear  +  adj.
```

financial (fə'nænʃəl) *adj.* 財務的

They're in *financial* difficulties now.

(88 南區四技夜二專)

foolish 〔'fulɪʃ 〕 *adj.* 愚蠢的

How *foolish* it is for you to walk in the rain.

（ 87 中區四技夜二專 ）

frozen 〔'frozn̩ 〕 *adj.* 冷凍的

That big grocery store sells a lot of *frozen* food. (78 四技商專)

fragrant 〔'fregrənt 〕 *adj.* 芳香的

The flower smells *fragrant*. (77 四技商專)

G g

gloomy 〔'glumɪ 〕 *adj.* 陰暗的

The cave was *gloomy* even in the daytime.

（ 80 彰化師大 ）

gossipy 〔'gɑsəpɪ 〕 *adj.* 愛說閒話的

Mrs. Jones is very *gossipy*. (78 師大工教)

自我測驗

- [ ] dull　　　　　＿＿＿＿＿＿＿＿
- [ ] eager　　　　　＿＿＿＿＿＿＿＿
- [ ] economic　　　＿＿＿＿＿＿＿＿
- [ ] elder　　　　　＿＿＿＿＿＿＿＿
- [ ] essential　　　＿＿＿＿＿＿＿＿

- [ ] evil　　　　　＿＿＿＿＿＿＿＿
- [ ] excellent　　　＿＿＿＿＿＿＿＿
- [ ] excited　　　　＿＿＿＿＿＿＿＿
- [ ] familar　　　　＿＿＿＿＿＿＿＿
- [ ] famous　　　　＿＿＿＿＿＿＿＿

- [ ] far　　　　　　＿＿＿＿＿＿＿＿
- [ ] fertile　　　　＿＿＿＿＿＿＿＿
- [ ] foolish　　　　＿＿＿＿＿＿＿＿
- [ ] frozen　　　　　＿＿＿＿＿＿＿＿
- [ ] gossipy　　　　＿＿＿＿＿＿＿＿

Check List

1. 懷疑的　　　　d ___doubtful___ l
2. 耐久的　　　　d _____ e
3. 渴望的　　　　e _____ r
4. 教育的　　　　e _____ l
5. 有效的　　　　e _____ e
6. 必要的　　　　e _____ l
7. 準確的　　　　e _____ t
8. 獨有的　　　　e _____ e
9. 筋疲力盡的　　e _____ d
10. 絕種的　　　　e _____ t
11. 有名的　　　　f _____ s
12. 最喜愛的　　　f _____ e
13. 財務的　　　　f _____ l
14. 芳香的　　　　f _____ t
15. 陰暗的　　　　g _____ y

greedy ('gridɪ) *adj.* 貪心的

It was *greedy* of you to take all of the cookies. (78 師大工教，88 北區四技夜二專)

guilty ('gɪltɪ) *adj.* 有罪的

Proved *guilty* of bribery, the official was soon sent to jail. (79 四技工專)

H h

hardworking ('hɑrd'wɝkɪŋ) *adj.* 努力的；用功的

Tom is a *hardworking* student. (78 四技工專)

harmonious (hɑr'monɪəs) *adj.* 和諧的；調和的

Physical education should aim at *harmonious* development of body and mind.

(83 四技商專、彰化師大)

hazardous 〔ˈhæzɚdəs〕 *adj.* 危險的

In many factories, especially the smaller ones, workers are working in poor and *hazardous* conditions. (84 保送甄試)

healthy 〔ˈhɛlθɪ〕 *adj.* 健康的

Everyone needs activities to develop a strong mind and a *healthy* body.

(77 保送甄試)

```
health + y
  |      |
 健康  + adj.
```

heavy 〔ˈhɛvɪ〕 *adj.* （交通）流量大的

The traffic was so *heavy* that it took us a long time to get there. (87 四技工專、師大工教)

herbal 〔ˈhɝbl̩〕 *adj.* 草藥的；草的

Herbal medicine and chemical medicine work side by side to give us long and healthy lives. (82 北區夜二專)

high 〔 haɪ 〕 *adj.* （評價）高的

We had a *high* opinion of the statesman.

（86 中區四技夜二專）

hostile 〔'hɑstɪl 〕 *adj.* 有敵意的

He is *hostile* to me.　He treats me as if I were his enemy.（80 四技工專）

human 〔'hjumən 〕 *adj.* 人類的

The Industrial Revolution is very significant in *human* history.（82 保送甄試）

humble 〔'hʌmbḷ 〕 *adj.* 謙虛的

To be *humble* towards your friends will help you succeed.（77 四技商專）

I i

identical 〔 aɪ'dɛntɪkḷ 〕 *adj.* 完全相同的

They look *identical* because they are twins.

（88 北區四技夜二專）

ignorant 〔'ɪgnərənt〕 *adj.* 不知道的

People living in cities for a long time are often completely *ignorant* of farm life.

（79 四技工專）

ill 〔 ɪl 〕 *adj.* 生病的

John was *ill* yesterday, so he didn't go to school. （85 四技工專、師大工教）

illegal 〔ɪ'ligḷ〕 *adj.* 非法的

It is *illegal* to own a gun in Taiwan.

（89 北區四技夜二專）

```
il  + legal
 |      |
not + 合法的
```

imaginable 〔ɪ'mædʒɪnəbḷ〕 *adj.* 可想像的

If we don't do it according to his plan, we shall have the greatest difficulty *imaginable*.

（77 台北夜二專，86 中區四技夜二專）

incapable〔ɪnˈkepəbḷ〕*adj.* 無能力的

I am *incapable* of solving this math problem without a calculator.（87四技商專、彰師商教）

indispensable〔ˌɪndɪsˈpɛnsəbḷ〕*adj.*
不可或缺的

Electrical energy is *indispensable* nowadays.

（78保送甄試，85保送甄試）

individual〔ˌɪndəˈvɪdʒuəl〕*adj.* 個別的

A good teacher should pay attention to students' *individual* differences.（89科大、四技工專）

industrial〔ɪnˈdʌstrɪəl〕*adj.* 工業的

People living in the *industrial* nations enjoy a better standard of living.

（79台北夜二專）

industr + ial
| |
工業   + *adj.*

industrialized ﹝ ɪn'dʌstrɪəl͵aɪzd ﹞ *adj.*
工業化的

With a skill or technique, a person finds
himself useful in an *industrialized* society.

（83 四技商專、彰化師大）

industrious ﹝ ɪn'dʌstrɪəs ﹞ *adj.* 勤勉的

Mr. Smith was *industrious*
in his own business.

（86 中區四技夜二專）

industr	+ ious
|	|
勤奮	+ *adj.*

ineffective ﹝͵ɪnə'fɛktɪv ﹞ *adj.* 無效的

Unfortunately, the new drug is *ineffective*
and does not prevent colds. （91 四技二專）

infectious ﹝ ɪn'fɛkʃəs ﹞ *adj.* 傳染性的

Measles is an *infectious* disease.

（87 四技商專、彰師商教）

in	+ fect	+ ious
|	|	|
in	+ *make*	+ *adj.*

 自我測驗

- [ ] greedy   _____
- [ ] guilty   _____
- [ ] hardworking   _____
- [ ] healthy   _____
- [ ] heavy   _____

- [ ] herbal   _____
- [ ] high   _____
- [ ] human   _____
- [ ] identical   _____
- [ ] ill   _____

- [ ] imaginable   _____
- [ ] individual   _____
- [ ] industrial   _____
- [ ] industrious   _____
- [ ] ineffective   _____

Check List

1. 有罪的　　　　g _____*guilty*_____ y
2. 和諧的　　　　h _____ s
3. 危險的　　　　h _____ s
4. 草　的　　　　h _____ l
5. 有敵意的　　　h _____ e
6. 謙虛的　　　　h _____ e
7. 完全相同的　　i _____ l
8. 不知道的　　　i _____ t
9. 非法的　　　　i _____ l
10. 無能力的　　　i _____ e
11. 不可或缺的　　i _____ e
12. 個別的　　　　i _____ l
13. 工業化的　　　i _____ d
14. 勤勉的　　　　i _____ s
15. 傳染性的　　　i _____ s

informal 〔 ɪnˋfɔrml̩ 〕 *adj.* 非正式的

Will the party be formal or *informal*?

（79 保送甄試）

informed 〔 ɪnˋfɔrmd 〕 *adj.* 消息靈通的

He is very well *informed* about the export market. （79 台北夜二專）

innocent 〔 ˋɪnəsn̩t 〕 *adj.* 無罪的

Every citizen has the right to be considered *innocent* in all criminal cases, unless proved otherwise. （84 四技商專、彰師商教）

insurable 〔 ɪnˋʃurəbl̩ 〕 *adj.* 可以保險的

Certain items are not *insurable* under any conditions. （78 師大工教）

interesting 〔 ˋɪntrɪstɪŋ 〕 *adj.* 有趣的

Ths story is very *interesting* to me. （80 師大工教）

international〔͵ɪntɚ'næʃənḷ〕 *adj.* 國際的

English has become a very important

international language. (83 北區夜二專，87 台北夜二專，

88 保送甄試、南區四技夜二專，90 科大、四技二專)

J j

jealous〔'dʒɛləs〕 *adj.* 嫉妒的

I often felt *jealous* because Peter could go

out when he wished. (81 四技商專)

L l

large〔lɑrdʒ〕 *adj.* 大的

Mr. Brown is a rich man and he bought a

large house a month ago. (85 四技工專、師大工教)

learned〔'lɝnɪd〕 *adj.* 有學問的

Brian is a scholar. Everyone considers him

learned. (87 保送甄試)

leisure 〔'liʒɚ〕 *adj.* 空閒的

I am so busy that I have no *leisure* time for sport. (88 科大、四技工專)

liberal 〔'lɪbərəl〕 *adj.* 文理科的

Literature, language, history, and philosophy are some of the *liberal* arts. (78 師大工教)

loose 〔lus〕 *adj.* 鬆的

Please make the belt tighter; it is too *loose* for comfort. (82 四技工專、師大工教)

lost 〔lɔst〕 *adj.* 迷路的

You have to ask for directions when you get *lost* in the city. (77 四技商專)

lunar 〔'lunɚ〕 *adj.* 農曆的；月亮的

Chinese farmers used to read the Chinese *lunar* calendar to see what weather and what fortune they might have. (88 中區四技夜二專)

M m

magnificent ﹝ mægˋnɪfəsn̩t ﹞ *adj.* 壯麗的

The mountains and lakes of Switzerland are beautiful. It is a country with *magnificent* scenery. (87 四技商專、彰師商教)

magn	+ ific	+ ent
great	+ make	+ adj.

man-made ﹝ˋmænˏmed ﹞ *adj.* 人造的

Chemists make different kinds of *man-made* material like plastic and nylon. (79 四技商專)

married ﹝ˋmærɪd ﹞ *adj.* 結婚的；已婚的

They plan to get *married* next month. (81 四技商專)

meaningful ﹝ˋminɪŋfəl ﹞ *adj.* 有意義的

In more *meaningful* terms, you can imagine an object traveling around the world in about 1/7 of a second. (79 台北夜二專)

measured ('mɛʒəd) *adj.* 慎重的

The angry old man spoke to the crowd in *measured* speech. (77 台北夜二專)

medical ('mɛdɪkl̩) *adj.* 醫學的

My mother is now under *medical* treatment in the hostipal. She is being treated with a new drug for diabetes. (89 北區四技夜二專)

middle ('mɪdl̩) *adj.* 中間的

Most Westerners' names consist of three parts, the first name, the *middle* name, and the last name. (87 中區四技夜二專)

monotonous (mə'natənəs) *adj.* 單調的

Hobbies provide variety for workers who do the same *monotonous* tasks all day long.

(82 北區夜二專)

mono	+ ton	+ ous
|	|	|
one	+ *tone*	+ *adj.*

mysterious 〔 mɪs'tɪrɪəs 〕 *adj.* 神秘的

Lightning was so *mysterious* to the ancient Greeks. (81 台北夜二專)

N n

native 〔'netɪv 〕 *adj.* 本國的

For most people living in the U.S., English is their *native* language. (89 技優保甄)

natural 〔'nætʃərəl 〕 *adj.* 自然的

Jimmy is interested in animals and wildflowers, so I'm sure he would enjoy this book on the *natural* history of Taiwan.

(79 師大工教，81 四技工專、師大工教)

natur	+	al
自然	+	*adj.*

# 自我測驗

- [ ] informal _____
- [ ] innocent _____
- [ ] interesting _____
- [ ] international _____
- [ ] jealous _____

- [ ] large _____
- [ ] liberal _____
- [ ] lost _____
- [ ] lunar _____
- [ ] man-made _____

- [ ] married _____
- [ ] measured _____
- [ ] middle _____
- [ ] native _____
- [ ] natural _____

 **Check List**

1. 非正式的　　i _____*informal*_____ l
2. 消息靈通的　i _____ d
3. 可以保險的　i _____ e
4. 嫉妒的　　　j _____ s
5. 有學問的　　l _____ d
6. 空閒的　　　l _____ e
7. 鬆　的　　　l _____ e
8. 農曆的　　　l _____ r
9. 壯麗的　　　m _____ t
10. 有意義的　　m _____ l
11. 慎重的　　　m _____ d
12. 醫學的　　　m _____ l
13. 單調的　　　m _____ s
14. 神秘的　　　m _____ s
15. 本國的　　　n _____ e

necessary 〔'nɛsə,sɛrɪ〕*adj.* 必需的

English, which is widely regarded as the global language, is *necessary* nowadays.

（90科大、四技二專）

negative 〔'nɛgətɪv〕*adj.* 消極的；否定的

It is difficult to be happy if you always have a *negative* attitude.

（89科大、四技簡專、農科）

```
nega  +  tive
 |        |
deny  +  adj.
```

neglectful 〔nɪ'glɛktfəl〕*adj.* 疏忽的

You shouldn't depend on him because he is often *neglectful* of his duties. （89四技二專）

nervous (ˈnɝvəs) *adj.* 緊張的

I always feel *nervous* before an important exam. (89 技優保甄)

```
nerv + ous
  |       |
神經  +  adj.
```

noted (ˈnotɪd) *adj.* 著名的

Woolen cloth has been a *noted* product of Great Britain for centuries. (78 四技商專)

nuclear (ˈnjuklɪɚ) *adj.* 核子的

Nuclear energy can be used to produce electricity. (88 中區四技夜二專)

numerous (ˈnjumərəs) *adj.* 許多的

There are *numerous* advantages to completing high school. (90 科大、四技工專)

O o

only (ˈonlɪ) *adj.* 唯一的

We were the *only* students in the class who could speak English. (79 師大工教)

optimistic 〔ˌɑptə'mɪstɪk〕 *adj.* 樂觀的

My father always holds an *optimistic* view of events. In other words, he hopes for the best.（86 四技商專、彰師商敎）

outgoing 〔'aʊtˌgoɪŋ〕 *adj.* 外向的

She is an active and *outgoing* girl.

（87 四技商專、彰師商敎）

outstanding 〔aʊt'stændɪŋ〕 *adj.* 傑出的

Michael was awarded a medal for his *outstanding* performance.（88 北區四技夜二專）

overconfident 〔'ovɚ'kɑnfədənt〕 *adj.* 過分自信的；自負的

Swimmers *overconfident* of their endurance often go out so far that they are too exhausted to return to the shore.（83 四技商專、彰化師大）

P p

panicky 〔'pænɪkɪ〕*adj.* 驚慌的

He was so *panicky* that he stood dumb with his mouth open. (81 台北夜二專)

particular 〔pə'tɪkjələ〕*adj.* 特別的

This breed of dog is generally aggressive, but this *particular* dog is very gentle.

(87 四技工專、師大工教，90 科大、四技工專)

patient 〔'peʃənt〕*adj.* 有耐心的

Jackson is not very *patient*; he doesn't like to wait for other people. (86 南區四技夜二專)

perfect 〔'pɝfɪkt〕*adj.* 完美的

Practice makes *perfect*. (82 嘉南、高屏區夜二專)

pessimistic 〔͵pɛsə'mɪstɪk〕*adj.* 悲觀的

He is such a *pessimistic* person that he
always thinks the worst is going to happen.

（91 四技二專）

pleasant 〔'plɛznt〕*adj.* 令人愉快的

The supermarket has a comfortable
temperature in summer, so it is a *pleasant*
place for people to stay and spend more
money.（80 師大工敎，82 四技商專、彰化師大）

pleased 〔plizd〕*adj.* 高興的；滿意的

I was *pleased* with his answers.

（85 四技工專、師大工敎）

polar 〔'polɚ〕*adj.* 極地的

The air in the *polar* regions is very cold and
dry.（87 保送甄試）

political 〔 pə'lɪtɪkl̩ 〕 *adj.* 政治上的

Political decisions have a widespread
impact on economic development. (85 保送甄試)

positive 〔'pɑzətɪv 〕 *adj.* 積極的；正面的

Be *positive*! You still have a chance to pass
the exam. (89 中區夜四技二專)

possible 〔'pɑsəbl̩ 〕 *adj.* 可能的

If *possible*, send it to my office tomorrow.

(87 中區四技夜二專)

potential 〔 pə'tɛnʃəl 〕 *adj.* 有潛力的

We are seen as *potential* consumers by
advertisers. (86 台北夜二專)

previous 〔'privɪəs 〕 *adj.* 之前的

I didn't like my *previous* job, so I quit it.

(88 北區四技夜二專)

自我測驗

- ☐ necessary   _____
- ☐ nervous   _____
- ☐ noted   _____
- ☐ only   _____
- ☐ outgoing   _____

- ☐ overconfident   _____
- ☐ particular   _____
- ☐ patient   _____
- ☐ perfect   _____
- ☐ pleasant   _____

- ☐ pleased   _____
- ☐ polar   _____
- ☐ positive   _____
- ☐ possible   _____
- ☐ previous   _____

1. 消極的　　　n ___negative___ e

2. 疏忽的　　　n _____ l

3. 核子的　　　n _____ r

4. 許多的　　　n _____ s

5. 樂觀的　　　o _____ c

6. 外向的　　　o _____ g

7. 傑出的　　　o _____ g

8. 驚慌的　　　p _____ y

9. 特別的　　　p _____ r

10. 有耐心的　　p _____ t

11. 悲觀的　　　p _____ c

12. 政治上的　　p _____ l

13. 積極的　　　p _____ e

14. 可能的　　　p _____ l

15. 之前的　　　p _____ s

professional 〔 prəˈfɛʃənḷ 〕 *adj.* 職業的

John is a *professional* tennis player; he plays tennis to make money. (80 台北夜二專)

promising 〔ˈprɑmɪsɪŋ 〕 *adj.* 有希望的

He has a *promising* future as a scientist.

(89 四技二專)

prospective 〔 prəˈspɛktɪv 〕 *adj.* 未來的；
可能的

He gave the *prospective* employer a good impression at the interview. (84 台北夜二專)

protective 〔 prəˈtɛktɪv 〕 *adj.* 保護的；
防護的

All the men working at the atomic power station have to be equipped with the *protective* clothes. (79 師大工教)

proud 〔praʊd〕 *adj.* 驕傲的；以～爲榮的

He is *proud* of his son. (77 保送甄試，83 保送甄試)

punctual 〔'pʌŋktʃʊəl〕 *adj.* 守時的

He comes at seven-thirty every morning
and this shows that he is *punctual*. (80 彰化師大)

R r

ready 〔'rɛdɪ〕 *adj.* 準備好的

He has studied very hard. Now he is *ready*
for the examination. (88 科大、四技工專)

reference 〔'rɛfrəns〕 *adj.* 參考用的

The dictionary is a very useful *reference*
book. (89 四技二專)

reliable 〔rɪ'laɪəbḷ〕 *adj.* 可靠的

Is the information you
gathered *reliable*?

(83 四技商專、彰化師大)

reli	+	able
|		|
rely	+	可以

religious ﹝ rɪˋlɪdʒəs ﹞ *adj.* 宗教的

Mary is a Christain. In other words,
Christanity is her *religious* belief.

（89中區夜四技二專）

reluctant ﹝ rɪˋlʌktənt ﹞ *adj.* 不情願的

My teacher was *reluctant* to let me take the
test again, but I finally persuaded her.

（91四技二專）

residential ﹝ ˏrɛzəˋdɛnʃəl ﹞ *adj.* 住宅的

Around the downtown area, there are
residential areas with houses and
apartments. （82保送甄試）

re	+ sid	+ ent	+ ial
back	+ *sit*	+ 人	+ *adj.* （回家坐下）

resistant 〔 rɪ'zɪstənt 〕 *adj.* 抵抗的；
有耐力的
Lead glass is very *resistant* to electricity, so
it is used in making television tubes and
insulators. (78 四技商專)

rich 〔 rɪtʃ 〕 *adj.* 豐富的
Most Arab countries are *rich* in oil.

(79 保送甄試，89 科大、四技工專)

ridiculous 〔 rɪ'dɪkjələs 〕 *adj.* 荒謬的；
可笑的
It is *ridiculous* to wear a raincoat on a
sunny day. (81 四技商專)

ripe 〔 raɪp 〕 *adj.* 成熟的
I can't eat this mango because it is not *ripe*
yet. (88 科大、四技工專)

rude 〔 rud 〕 *adj.* 無禮的
It is *rude* to ask someone to do something
without saying "please." (87 中區四技夜二專)

S s

sad 〔 sæd 〕 *adj.* 悲傷的

Peter felt very *sad* when his father died.

（81 四技工專、師大工教）

satisfactory 〔 ͵sætɪsˈfæktərɪ 〕 *adj.* 令人滿意的

What he has done is quite *satisfactory* to me.

（78 保送甄試，81 台北夜二專）

scared 〔 skɛrd 〕 *adj.* 害怕的

When Mary saw the big dog, she was very *scared*. （82 嘉南、高屏區夜二專）

sensitive 〔ˈsɛnsətɪv 〕 *adj.* 敏感的

A decayed tooth is very *sensitive* to heat and cold. （78 師大工教）

sens + ible
| |
feel + *adj.*

serious 〔'sɪrɪəs 〕 *adj.* 嚴重的

He made a *serious* mistake. He just erased all our computer records. (81 四技工專、師大工敎)

serviceable 〔'sɝvɪsəbḷ 〕 *adj.* 耐用的

Cotton twill is a *serviceable* material.

(77 台北夜二專)

shabby 〔'ʃæbɪ 〕 *adj.* 衣衫襤褸的

He looked rather *shabby* in those clothes. He was not decently dressed. (77 師大工敎)

significant 〔 sɪg'nɪfəkənt 〕 *adj.* 意義重大的

Dr. Sun Yet-sen made a *significant* contribution to our country. (80 四技商專)

sign	+	ific	+	ant
mark	+	make	+	adj. (做出記號)

 **自我測驗**

- ☐ professional _____
- ☐ promising _____
- ☐ prospective _____
- ☐ proud _____
- ☐ ready _____

- ☐ reliable _____
- ☐ religious _____
- ☐ resistant _____
- ☐ rich _____
- ☐ ripe _____

- ☐ rude _____
- ☐ sad _____
- ☐ scared _____
- ☐ serious _____
- ☐ shabby _____

 **Check List**

1. 有希望的　　p <u>*promising*</u> g

2. 保護的　　　p _____ e

3. 守時的　　　p _____ l

4. 參考用的　　r _____ e

5. 可靠的　　　r _____ e

6. 不情願的　　r _____ t

7. 住宅的　　　r _____ l

8. 抵抗的　　　r _____ t

9. 荒謬的　　　r _____ s

10. 成熟的　　　r _____ e

11. 令人滿意的　s _____ y

12. 害怕的　　　s _____ d

13. 敏感的　　　s _____ e

14. 耐用的　　　s _____ e

15. 意義重大的　s _____ t

single ('sɪŋgl̩) *adj.* 單人的；單一的

Excuse me. Do you have a *single* room available tonight? (82 嘉南、高屏區夜二專)

sleepy ('slipɪ) *adj.* 想睡的

A lot of students feel *sleepy* during a lengthy speech. (87 中區四技夜二專)

slender ('slɛndɚ) *adj.* 苗條的

One of the twins is *slender*, but the other is overweight. (89 科大、四技商專、農科)

sloppy ('slɑpɪ) *adj.* 邋遢的

Joe is so *sloppy* that his room is always a mess. (89 科大、四技商專、農專)

soaked (sokt) *adj.* 溼透的

To avoid catching a cold, you had better change your *soaked* clothes.

(89 科大、四技商專、農專)

solar 〔'solɚ〕 *adj.* 太陽的

Solar energy released from the sun does not cause any pollution. (79 四技工專，87 保送甄試)

social 〔'soʃəl〕 *adj.* 社會的

During the Chou dynasty the Chinese set up a government system and established many *social* customs. (88 中區四技夜二專)

sophisticated 〔sə'fɪstɪˌketɪd〕 *adj.*

精密的；複雜的

People now are looking for *sophisticated* but easy-to-use equipment. (89 四技二專)

soph + ist + icated
wise + 人 + *adj.*

specific ﹝ spɪˈsɪfɪk ﹞ *adj.* 明確的

An invitation should be *specific* and give time, place and purpose of meeting.

（81 台北夜二專）

```
spec  + ific
  |       |
 see   + adj. (看得出來的)
```

splendid ﹝ˈsplɛndɪd﹞ *adj.* 極好的

My teacher said I had done a *splendid* job and gave me an A. （89 科大、四技簡專、農科）

stationary ﹝ˈsteʃənˌɛrɪ﹞ *adj.* 固定的

If you have a *stationary* bicycle, you can exercise in your own home. （88 保送甄試）

stimulative ﹝ˈstɪmjəˌletɪv﹞ *adj.* 激勵的

Our government has adopted *stimulative* measures to speed up economic recovery.

（78 台北夜二專）

straight 〔 stret 〕 *adj.* 直的

Keep you back *straight* （88科大、四技工專）

strange 〔 stredʒ 〕 *adj.* 奇怪的

I observed something *strange* in his behavior.

（80 保送甄試）

strong 〔 strɔŋ 〕 *adj.* 強壯的

Exercise keeps our body *strong*. （79 保送甄試）

subject 〔'sʌbdʒɪkt 〕 *adj.* 須服從～的

We are *subject* to the laws of our country.

（78 保送甄試）

suitable 〔'sutəbḷ 〕 *adj.* 適當的

Christina is doubtless the most *suitable* person for that promising job. She has work experience and the personality to succeed.

（83 保送甄試）

sunburned (ˈsʌnˌbɝnd) *adj.* 曬黑的

If your skin is exposed to the sunlight for a long time in summer, you'll get *sunburned*.

（86 保送甄試）

surgical (ˈsɝdʒɪkḷ) *adj.* 外科的

The old doctor has much *surgical* experience. （78 台北夜二專）

surprised (səˈpraɪzd) *adj.* 感到驚訝的

There is nothing to be *surprised* at.

（78 台北夜二專）

swollen (ˈswolən) *adj.* 腫脹的

When selecting canned goods, never buy cans that have *swollen* ends. （84 四技商專、彰師商教）

symbolic (sɪmˈbɑlɪk) *adj.* 象徵的

A dove is *symbolic* of peace. （77 台北夜二專）

T t

tedious ('tidɪəs) *adj.* 乏味的

A long, dull speech is *tedious*. (79 四技工專)

temporary ('tɛmpə,rɛrɪ) *adj.* 暫時的

I plan to find a *temporary* job during the
summer vacation. (81 台北夜二專)

terrified ('tɛrə,faɪd) *adj.* 感到害怕的

Little children are easily *terrified* by loud
sounds. (88 四技商專)

tropical ('trɑpɪkḷ) *adj.* 熱帶的

The temperatures in *tropical* regions are
high all the year round.

(87 保送甄試，89 中區夜四技二專)

# 自我測驗

- ☐ sleepy _____
- ☐ slender _____
- ☐ sloppy _____
- ☐ soaked _____
- ☐ social _____

- ☐ specific _____
- ☐ stationary _____
- ☐ stimulative _____
- ☐ straight _____
- ☐ subject _____

- ☐ suitable _____
- ☐ surgical _____
- ☐ surprised _____
- ☐ tedious _____
- ☐ terrified _____

1. 單人的   s _____*single*_____ e
2. 苗條的   s _____ r
3. 溼透的   s _____ d
4. 精密的   s _____ d
5. 明確的   s _____ c

6. 極好的   s _____ d
7. 激勵的   s _____ e
8. 奇怪的   s _____ e
9. 強壯的   s _____ g
10. 適合的   s _____ e

11. 曬黑的   s _____ d
12. 腫脹的   s _____ n
13. 象徵的   s _____ c
14. 暫時的   t _____ y
15. 熱帶的   t _____ l

U u

unfermented 〔͵ʌnfɚˈmɛntɪd〕*adj.* 未發酵的

Green tea is simply *unfermented* tea and it contains a lot of vitamin C. （89中區夜四技二專）

unnecessary 〔ʌnˈnɛsə͵sɛrɪ〕*adj.* 不必要的

We should turn off *unnecessary* lights to save electricity. （82嘉南、高屏區夜二專）

urban 〔ˈɝbən〕*adj.* 都市的

Most people in Taiwan live in an *urban* area.

（88北區四技夜二專）

urgent 〔ˈɝdʒənt〕*adj.* 緊急的

Please send this letter as quickly as possible; it's very *urgent*. （86南區四技夜二專）

useful ('jusfəl) *adj.* 有用的

The dictionary is very *useful* to a
language learner.

(86 四技工專、師大工教，90 科大、四技工專)

```
use  + ful
 |      |
用   + adj.
```

V v

vacant ('vekənt) *adj.* 空的

This apartment has been *vacant* for three
months. (89 四技二專)

valuable ('væljuəb!) *adj.* 有價值的

Gold is a *valuable* metal. (77 四技工專)

various ('vɛrɪəs) *adj.* 各式各樣的

Today more women are working in *various*
fields. (87 南區四技夜二專)

```
vari   + ous
 |        |
change + adj.
```

vending (ˈvɛndɪŋ) *adj.* 出售的

You can buy drinks from the *vending* machines in the hallway. (88 科大、四技工專)

vocational (voˈkeʃənḷ) *adj.* 職業的

Would you like to study in a technical or a *vocational* school? (87 南區四技夜二專)

W w

weak (wik) *adj.* 虛弱的

Mr. Brown is so *weak* that he can't even stand up. (86 四技工專、師大工教)

whole (hol) *adj.* 整個的

Yesterday I spent the *whole* night studying math. (89 中區夜四技二專)

wide (waɪd) *adj.* 寬的

The bridge is *wide* enough for six lanes of cars, three in each direction. (79 保送甄試)

副 詞

absolutely (ˈæbsəˌlutlɪ) *adv.* 絕對地；
完全地

I am *absolutely* sure that I locked the door;
there is no doubt in my mind. (89科大、四技簡專、農專)

accordingly (əˈkɔrdɪŋlɪ) *adv.* 因此

He had loved her and he had been,
accordingly, good to her. (81四技簡專)

actually (ˈæktʃuəlɪ) *adv.* 實際上

Actually, I can't afford the house because it
is too expensive. (83保送甄試)

adequately (ˈædəkwɪtlɪ) *adv.* 充分地

He was not *adequately* dressed for the winter
weather and felt cold. (88四技二專)

aloud 〔ə'laʊd〕 *adv.* 大聲地

Reading *aloud* may help you improve your pronunciation. (89 技優保甄)

ambitiously 〔æm'bɪʃəslɪ〕 *adv.* 有野心地；有抱負地

The young man has always worked *ambitiously*. (80 師大工教)

automatically 〔ˌɔtə'mætɪklɪ〕 *adv.* 自動地

A robot is a device that can do certain jobs *automatically*. (87 四技工專、師大工教)

C c

carefully 〔'kɛrfəlɪ〕 *adv.* 小心地

We have to choose friends *carefully*.

(86 四技工專、師大工教)

confidentially (ˌkɑnfəˈdɛnʃəlɪ) *adv.*
秘密地;偷偷地

He talked to me about the problem
confidentially, so I can't tell you what he said.

(89 科大、四技商專、農科)

D d

deeply (ˈdiplɪ) *adv.* 深深地;強烈地

Every guest at the party was *deeply*
impressed with Mr. Stone's hospitality.

(84 四技商專、彰師商教)

domestically (dəˈmɛstɪklɪ) *adv.*
在國內

When a nation lacks resources needed to
produce goods *domestically*, it may import
them from another country. (83 四技商專、彰化師大)

- ☐ unfermented _____
- ☐ urban _____
- ☐ vacant _____
- ☐ valuable _____
- ☐ vending _____

- ☐ vocational _____
- ☐ whole _____
- ☐ accordingly _____
- ☐ actually _____
- ☐ adequately _____

- ☐ aloud _____
- ☐ automatically _____
- ☐ carefully _____
- ☐ confidentially _____
- ☐ domestically _____

Check List

1. 不必要的   u _unnecessary_ y

2. 都市的   u _____ n

3. 有用的   u _____ l

4. 空　的   v _____ t

5. 各式各樣的   v _____ s

6. 職業的   v _____ l

7. 虛弱的   w _____ k

8. 寬　的   w _____ e

9. 絕對地   a _____ y

10. 因　此   a _____ y

11. 充分地   a _____ y

12. 有野心地   a _____ y

13. 秘密地   c _____ y

14. 深深地   d _____ y

15. 在國內   d _____ y

destructively 〔 dɪˈstrʌktɪvlɪ 〕 *adv.*

破壞性地

The youths behaved *destructively* at the
concert, causing a great deal of damage.

（87 保送甄試）

discreetly 〔 dɪˈskritlɪ 〕 *adv.* 謹慎地

I told my father *discreetly* that he was talking
too loudly. （89 科大、四技商專、農專）

E e

easily 〔ˈizɪlɪ 〕 *adv.* 容易地

Copper and aluminum can be bent *easily* to
any shape. （78 四技商專）

easi	+	ly
容易的	+	*adv.*

enormously 〔 ɪˈnɔrməslɪ 〕 *adv.* 巨大地

The political situation of the world has
changed *enormously* during recent years.

（87 四技商專、彰師商教）

entirely 〔 ɪnˈtaɪrlɪ 〕 adv. 完全地

We got lost because your directions were
not *entirely* correct. (89 四技二專)

eventually 〔 ɪˈvɛntʃʊəlɪ 〕 adv. 最後

You will be as tall as your father *eventually*.

(89 四技二專)

exactly 〔 ɪgˈzæktlɪ 〕 adv. 準確地；正好

The train arrived at *exactly* eight o'clock,
neither earlier nor later. (79 四技商專)

F f

fairly 〔ˈfɛrlɪ 〕 adv. 公平地

The judges reached their decision *fairly*.

(88 四技二專)

faithfully 〔ˈfeθfəlɪ 〕 adv. 忠實地

George comes to class *faithfully* every
Saturday. (89 科大、四技商專、農專)

finally (ˈfaɪn̩lɪ) *adv.* 最後；終於

I waited for two hours and he came *finally*.

（85 四技工專、師大工教）

fortunately (ˈfɔtʃənɪtlɪ) *adv.* 幸運地

My alarm clock did not go off but, *fortunately*, I was not late for school.

（86 保送甄試）

G g

genuinely (ˈdʒɛnjʊɪnlɪ) *adv.* 眞正地

Though a member of the royal family, Princess Diana was not *genuinely* happy in her lifetime. （89 科大、四技商專、農專）

H h

hardly (ˈhɑrdlɪ) *adv.* 幾乎不

Her bedroom was so small that she could *hardly* move in it. （81、88 四技商專）

I i

immediately 〔 ɪ'midɪɪtlɪ 〕 *adv.* 立刻

You should go and look for him *immediately*.

（80 四技商專，85 台北夜二專，85 四技工專、師大工教）

incredibly 〔 ɪn'krɛdəblɪ 〕 *adv.* 令人難以置信地

Incredibly, the man denied having stolen the car after he was caught driving. （86 保送甄試）

inevitably 〔 ɪn'ɛvətəblɪ 〕 *adv.* 不可避免地

He didn't work hard enough for the test; *inevitably*, he failed to pass it. （86 保送甄試）

instead 〔 ɪn'stɛd 〕 *adv.* 作爲替代

When he goes on a trip, he carries a credit card *instead* of large sums of cash.

（87 中區四技夜二專）

intimately （ˈɪntəmɪtlɪ ） *adv.* 親密地

I am acquainted with Tim, but I don't know him *intimately*. (88 四技二專)

irritably （ˈɪrətəblɪ ） *adv.* 暴躁地

John answered me *irritably* when I told him it was time to wake up. (89 北區四技夜二專)

M m

mainly （ˈmenlɪ ） *adv.* 主要地

French is spoken *mainly* in France. (79 四技商專)

medically （ˈmɛdɪklɪ ） *adj.* 醫學地；醫療地

The doctor found that he had high blood pressure and should be treated *medically*.

(89 北區四技夜二專)

N n

namely 〔'nemlɪ 〕 *adv.* 也就是

Six percent of the fifty students in this class are absent today; *namely*, three students are absent today. (86 保送甄試)

nowadays 〔'nauə,dez 〕 *adv.* 現今

Air pollution is one of the most important problems in Taiwan *nowadays*. (87 南區四技夜二專)

O o

obviously 〔'abvɪəslɪ 〕 *adv.* 顯然

He is *obviously* guilty of the theft because he is holding the stolen TV. (89 科大、四技商專、農專)

originally 〔 ə'rɪdʒənlɪ 〕 *adv.* 起初

Originally he planned to come but then he changed his mind.

(80 四技商專)

origin	+	al	+	ly
|		|		|
起源	+	*adj.*	+	*adv.*

自我測驗

- ☐ discreetly _____
- ☐ easily _____
- ☐ entirely _____
- ☐ fairly _____
- ☐ faithfully _____

- ☐ genuinely _____
- ☐ hardly _____
- ☐ incredibly _____
- ☐ inevitably _____
- ☐ intimately _____

- ☐ irritably _____
- ☐ namely _____
- ☐ nowadays _____
- ☐ obviously _____
- ☐ orignially _____

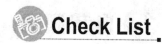 **Check List**

1. 破壞性地　　d _destructively_　y
2. 巨大地　　　e _____　y
3. 準確地　　　e _____　y
4. 忠實地　　　f _____　y
5. 最　後　　　f _____　y

6. 幸運地　　　f _____　y
7. 立　刻　　　i _____　y
8. 作為替代　　i _____　d
9. 親密地　　　i _____　y
10. 暴躁地　　　i _____　y

11. 主要地　　　m _____　y
12. 醫學地　　　m _____　y
13. 現　今　　　n _____　s
14. 顯　然　　　o _____　y
15. 起　初　　　o _____　y

P p

partly 〔'partlɪ 〕 *adv.* 部分地

The weather forecast for today is *partly* cloudy skies with only a small chance of rain.

（88 科大、四技工專）

permanently 〔'pɝmənəntlɪ 〕 *adv.* 永久地

Mr. Brown has been *permanently* assigned to teach our class. （87 保送甄試）

positively 〔'pazətɪvlɪ 〕 *adv.* 積極地；正面地

Paul always thinks *positively*. He believes in optimism. （88 四技商專）

possibly 〔'pasəblɪ 〕 *adv.* （能否）設法

Could you *possibly* come and stay with us some time during the holidays?

（88 中區四技夜二專）

pretty 〔'prɪtɪ〕 *adv.* 非常地

It's *pretty* hot today. (88 南區四技夜二專)

R r

regretfully 〔rɪ'grɛtfəlɪ〕 *adv.* 後悔地

Bill told me *regretfully* that he would not be able to come to the party. (87 四技工專、師大工教)

S s

seldom 〔'sɛldəm〕 *adv.* 很少

He often eats in a restaurant because his wife *seldom* cooks. (77 師大工教)

superstitiously 〔ˌsupɚ'stɪʃəslɪ〕 *adv.* 迷信地

He *superstitiously* believes that black cats are bad luck. (88 四技二專)

U u

unexpectedly 〔͵ʌnɪkˈspɛktɪdlɪ〕 *adv.*
意想不到地

While hunting on a rainy day, I was attacked
by a bear *unexpectedly*. (89 科大、四技簡專、農專)

urgently 〔ˈɝdʒəntlɪ〕 *adv.* 迫切地

Please dispatch the first part of this order
by air now, as these are *urgently* required
by customers. (79 四技簡專)

W w

widely 〔ˈwaɪdlɪ〕 *adv.* 廣泛地

It is *widely* known that Mr. Wang is a great
poet. (78 四技簡專)

★ 單字索引 ★

劉毅英文家教班高二、高三班
招生簡章

- **招生對象**：高二、高三同學

- **上課日期**：全年無休，天天有班

- **開課班級**：(為保障教學品質，額滿不收。)

A 班	週三晚上 6：00～9：30
B 班	週四晚上 6：00～9：30
C 班	週五晚上 6：00～9：30
D 班	週六上午 8：20～12：20
E 班	週六下午 1：20～5：20
F 班	週六晚上 6：00～9：30
G 班	週日上午 8：20～12：20
H 班	週日下午 1：20～5：20
I 班	週日晚上 6：00～9：30
J 班	週一晚上 6：00～9：30
K 班	週二晚上 6：00～9：30
N 班	週五晚上 6：00～9：30
O 班	週六上午 8：20～12：20
P 班	週六下午 1：20～5：20
Q 班	週六晚上 6：00～9：30
R 班	週日上午 8：20～12：20
S 班	週日下午 1：20～5：20

- **教學目標**：

　　　今年大學入學考試和以往不同，同學要考「**學科能力測驗**」，到了 7 月份，又要考「**大學入學指定科目考試**」，歷屆學科能力測驗已經考了 10 年了 (83～92 年)，題目比聯考簡單，但字數多達七頁，此項考試只是跨過門檻的考試，而

7月份的「指定科目考科」是要鑑別考生前面 60 %～70 %的能力，所以試題比大學聯考稍難，根據命題原則，單作文一項就要求達到 120～150 字，單字出題範圍在教育部所規定的常用七千個字彙內。面臨此一變換，我們有完全的準備，應付今年「指定科目考試」的七種題型命題，同學只要每週準時來上課，英文這一科交給「劉毅英文」，我們用簡單的方法，考試、背書、舉行各種比賽。無論如何，到了大考時，你的英文成績就會遠遠超過其他同學。

今年大學聯考，本班英文成績就是最好的證明，有哪一家補習班有我們四分之一好？他們連榜單都不敢公佈，為什麼？因為只有我們的「背書制度」和「模考制度」有效果。

- 獎學金制度：

  1. 凡報名後，過去在學校，高二上學期或高二下學期，在班上總成績，只要有一次前三名，就可申請一次獎學金，第一名 *3000* 元，第二名 *1000* 元，第三名 *1000* 元。
     （每人限領一次。）
  2. 高三同學上學期學校模擬考，只要有任何一次，英文成績在班上第一名的同學，就可得獎學金 *3000* 元。
     （每人限領一次。）
  3. 本班學期總成績，第一名 *10000* 元，第二名 *9000* 元，第三名 *8000* 元，第四名 *7000* 元，第五名 *5000* 元，以下略。
  4. 指定考科成績全國英文最高分，可得獎學金壹拾萬元；96 分以上，獎學金 *20000* 元；90 分以上，獎學金 *10000* 元；80 分以上 *1000* 元；60 分以上者，均有獎勵。
     （只限高三下學期補習同學。）

劉毅英文家教班（國一、國二、國三、高一、高二、高三班）

班址：台北市重慶南路一段 10 號 7F（火車站前・消防隊斜對面）

☎（02）2381-3148・2331-8822

全國第一次高職同學單字背誦比賽

I. **比賽宗旨：** 用比賽的方法，激勵同學背英文單字，同學可以在短時間內，增加英文的實力。這是訓練你記憶力和毅力最好的方法。背單字是學好英文的第一步，不管你將來升學或不升學，背英文單字會使你精神煥發，沒有煩惱，對未來充滿信心。

II. **背誦教材：** 學習出版公司最新出版，「四技二專 1000 字」（周岳曇主編），這是全國第一本電腦統計，最常考的字彙。同學背完以後，不僅考四技二專沒問題，對於考大學，以及中級英文檢定，也有所幫助。

III. **比賽資格：** 全國高職同學。

IV. **收費標準：** 報名費 200 元（報名後贈送「四技二專 1000 字」一本，如果已在市面購買，可憑發票及書籍，免費報名。）

V. **比賽辦法：** 可將「四技二專 1000 字」分次到櫃檯接受口試，導師說出中文，同學可唸出英文，並拼出該字的英文字母，錯誤不得超過 1 個以上，及算通過。

VI. **獎勵辦法：** 凡是優先背好前 200 名同學，可得獎金 *1000* 元。201～500 名，可得獎金 *500* 元。得獎同學將有工讀的機會。

VII. **口試地點：** 台北市重慶南路一段 10 號 7 F（劉毅英文家教班）

VIII. **口試時間：** 週一至週五下午 3：00～晚上 10：00
週六、週日及假日上午 8：00～晚上 10：00

||||||||||||||● 學習出版公司門市部 ● ||||||||||||||||

台北地區：台北市許昌街 10 號 2 樓　TEL：(02)2331-4060‧2331-9209
台中地區：台中市綠川東街 32 號 8 樓 23 室　TEL：(04)2223-2838

||||||||||||||||||||||||||||||||||||||||||||||||||||||||||||||||

四技二專 1000 字

主　　　編 / 周 岳 曇
發　行　所 / 學習出版有限公司　☎ (02) 2704-5525
郵 撥 帳 號 / 0512727-2 學習出版社帳戶
登　記　證 / 局版台業 2179 號
印　刷　所 / 裕強彩色印刷有限公司
台 北 門 市 / 台北市許昌街 10 號 2 F
　　　　　　☎ (02) 2331-4060‧2331-9209
台 中 門 市 / 台中市綠川東街 32 號 8 F 23 室　☎ (04) 2223-2838
台灣總經銷 / 紅螞蟻圖書有限公司　　☎ (02) 2795-3656
美國總經銷 / Evergreen Book Store　　☎ (818) 2813622
本公司網址　www.learnbook.com.tw
電 子 郵 件　learnbook@learnbook.com.tw

售價：新台幣二百二十元正

2003 年 4 月 1 日一版二刷

ISBN 957-519-672-4